GRAVITY

Advance Praise for *Gravity*

"A spicy novel about two young women daring to fly free in life and love while accurately depicting the thrill of ski jumping!" —Sarah Hendrickson, Olympic Ski Jumper and member of the US Ski Team Women's Ski Jumping Team

"Filled with vivid imagery—from describing the heat between the sheets to the cold of ski jump slopes—coupled with teen girls leaping deeply into love, betrayal, and the chasm between, Rich's frequently funny and sometime philosophical novel *Gravity* soars."—Patrick Jones, author of *Chasing Tail Lights*, Minnesota Book Award runner-up

"Juliann Rich has taken as much care in crafting *Gravity* as Ellie has taken in honing her sport of ski jumping and exacting revenge on her ex. *Gravity* is the intriguing tale of old love, new love, losses and gains. Rich executes an intense inrun, a brilliant take-off, a demanding freefall, and a graceful landing with this novel. If storytelling were an Olympic event, and I were a judge, I'd award *Gravity* a perfect 10."—Eva Indigo, author of *Tilt-a-Whirl* and *Laughing Down the Moon*

Visit us at www.boldstrokesbooks.com

By the Author

Caught in the Crossfire

Searching for Grace

Taking the Stand

Gravity

GRAVITY

by
Juliann Rich

2016

GRAVITY

ISBN 13: 978-1-62639-483-4

This Trade Paperback Original Is Published By
Bold Strokes Books, Inc.
P.O. Box 249
Valley Falls, NY 12185

First Edition: November 2016

CREDITS
Editors: Lynda Sandoval and Ruth Sternglantz
Production Design: Susan Ramundo
Cover Design By Sheri (graphicartist2020@hotmail.com)

Acknowledgments

Sometimes love wells up in an author and a book is born, written for her mother and dedicated to her son. Sometimes inspiration (or a previously conceived character) hounds an author to write a second and then a third book and a trilogy is born.

Sometimes, thankfully not often, a perfect storm hits an author's life and the ensuing pain spills onto the page, leading the author by the magic of the written word not only through her pain but toward healing.

That is how *Gravity* was born.

And so…I thank the storm. Yes, I thank the storm because it changed me and I like this version of Juliann a whole lot more than the previous one. I didn't write *Gravity* through the lens of a PFLAG Mom or as the daughter of missionaries. I wrote it from my heart, my broken heart, as I evolved into a woman of strength who asks for no permission to take up space in this world and speak my truth. Ellie Engebretsen and Kate Moreau, the women with whom I shared headspace for over a year, forged the path I needed to follow.

I also thank the women in my life who walked through the storm with me. Katie, Jennifer, Mary, Natalie, Laura, and Alexa, you made Wednesday my favorite day of the week. And George? You may not be a woman, but I'm including you in this thank you because none of us could have walked the storms of our lives without you.

As always, I am grateful to my team at Bold Strokes Books— Len Barot, Sandy Lowe, Lynda Sandoval, and Ruth Sternglantz. You granted me the time I needed to find my way through this story and the freedom to allow it to change and grow until it was not the book I'd promised I'd write for you, but the book I needed to write for myself. No artist could ask for more.

You see, initially I conceived *Gravity* to be a fun romance set against the thrilling backdrop of the ski jumping world. As a skier, I know the sting of the cold wind on my face, the pull of gravity that can be my best friend as I fly down a mountain or my worst enemy as I lie in a crumpled heap halfway down. Even as I write this, I can feel my boots biting into the back of my calves, telling me to slow down before I forget to thank someone who absolutely must be included in this acknowledgement.

Sarah Hendrickson.

Sarah is an Olympic Ski Jumper and member of the US Women's Ski Jumping team. She also holds the honor of being the first woman in history to ever ski jump in the Olympics, which occurred in Sochi in 2014. But that's not the thing that impresses me the most about Sarah. Not even close. When I reached out to Sarah, I hoped she might be willing to answer three or four questions. It was important, you see, for me to depict the world of ski jumping accurately, and I wanted to make sure I got the details right. Sarah not only answered those questions, she offered to read *Gravity*—in its entirety—and share her insider's perspective with me. Her praise of *Gravity* is on the back cover, and it's one of the coolest things that has ever happened to me in my career as an author. Sarah, thank you. *Gravity* would not be the book it is without your generous guidance.

I also want to thank Saritza Hernández, friend and agent. You believed in me when I didn't.

And I want to thank the PantyLiners, my writer's group: Aren Sabers, Heather Anastasiu, Rachel Gold, Dawn Klehr, Eva Indigo, and Vee Signorelli. You listened when I cried and then kicked me in the butt (lovingly) when the time for tears had passed and the time for writing had dawned. Because of you I found *my* voice, not as a mom or as a daughter, but as an author and as a woman. Because of you, *Gravity* was restored to my life.

Sammy, friend, son of my heart, giver of hugs... J. Leigh Bailey, agent mate, sharer of giggles, fellow Boy's Town and Navy Pier explorer...thank you both for being there for me throughout it all.

And finally, Jeff, I want to thank you, too. Yes, I do. Because despite it all, you remain my inspiration.

Dedication

This book is specifically dedicated to Sarah Hendrickson
and all the other members—past and present—
of the US Women's Ski Jumping Team,
who fought for their rightful place at the Olympics.
But it was also written for every woman who has
ever dared to fly free and been caught in Gravity's pull.

PROLOGUE

This is not a story about a girl who found the courage to come out as gay.

Wrong girl. Wrong book.

Sorry. (Not really.)

This is a story about a ski jumper—me. And an auburn-haired girl—Kate. And the biggest jump of all.

Ask any ski jumper and they'll tell you a truth that never airs on ESPN.

None of us jumps for the judges. Or the scores. Or to nail some fucking form.

We jump for those four, five, six seconds of airtime. Against the rush of the wind, despite the hard ground beneath us, we jump.

And in the jumping, we fly free.

So no, this isn't a story about a girl who found the courage to come out as gay.

Wrong girl. Wrong book.

Sorry. (Not really.)

This *is* a story about a girl who found the courage to jump, to fly, and—for a brief, precious time—to be free.

But here's the thing.

All flights come to an end.

Ask any ski jumper and they'll tell you that's another truth that never airs on ESPN.

For better. For worse. Gravity always wins.

PART I: THE INRUN

It's all about resistance.
Until it's not.

CHAPTER ONE

I need to throw myself off a mountain. I need to push myself until the only pain I have is in my body. That pain, I know. That pain, I can handle. Unfortunately, all I've got is Freefall, a steep vertical wall covered in ice and snow on the sheer north face of Moose Mountain at Lutsen resort. It's a Minnesota mountain. In other words, a glorified hill, but it will have to do.

Freefall.

I stab the snow with my poles and laugh aloud, an angry burst of breath crystallizing in the night air.

The price of falling is never free.

A girl in a pale blue jacket and rented skis zooms past me without pausing long enough to take in the view or assess the danger. Happens every year during the week between Christmas and New Year's. Some dumb tourist gets lost or cocky and tackles a black diamond run. It never ends well, but it does keep the ski patrol employed.

I aim my left ski straight down and, in one fluid motion, push against my poles and kick off with my right ski. The black-green blur of the evergreen trees to my right and left pick up speed as I do. Stark against the snow and strong, they refuse to shed so much as one needle in the cold-ass Minnesota winter.

The text. The text. The goddamn text. Never meant for my eyes. Impossible to forget.

Be an evergreen, I blink and tell myself. *Shed nothing.*

But I'm not an evergreen and the stinging hotness edges down my cheek where it freezes, an icy pimple of pain, and eventually falls onto the snow beneath me. I'm used to leaving a bit of myself on the slopes, but not like this.

Enough!

Crying over a broken heart is for the girls who count calories, not push-ups. Girls who drink lattes, not whiskey shots. Girls who spend their Sundays in the mall, not throwing themselves down ice-covered mountains. I plant my pole and kick against the beaten-down bed of snow, promising myself that the frozen tear, now forever a part of Freefall, is the last I will shed for Blair.

Ahead of me I spot the girl in the blue jacket. She's crouched low, head tucked, like she's in some goddamn hurry to have her death wish come true. Fucking idiot. Freefall isn't for skiers who want a vacation break from their lives. Freefall is for people who need to face death to feel alive.

The girl in the blue jacket is coming up on Freefall's rough patch where rocks jut out without warning. To make it worse I'm not seeing the sparkle of diamonds in the snow that indicates fresh powder. I'm seeing a flat whitish-blue patch that means only one thing. Ice.

"Oh, shit," I say, my boots biting into my calves as I try to slow down. This girl doesn't know she's about five seconds away from having a search and rescue party thrown in her honor as she hits the ice patch at full speed. I cringe, but then she's cutting through it with sharp left and right turns, leaning forward (forward!) until she clears it and reaches the bottom. She doesn't stop there to catch her breath or count her blessings or scratch off one of her nine lives. Most skiers have nothing left when they hit the bottom of Freefall and have to ice skate Valley Run, the trail that leads to the front of Moose Mountain, but not this girl. She harnesses her momentum and lets it propel her over Valley Run until she disappears from sight.

Well, shit. No way am I letting a girl like that ski my mountain without at least knowing her name. I bury my poles in my armpits and crouch low for maximum speed. The broken crusts of ice, compliments of mystery girl, are annoying but nothing I can't handle, and when I hit the bottom of Freefall, I, too, fly onto Valley Run, my eyes searching for a bit of pale blue until I spot her already standing in line for the lift that leads to Eagle Ridge. Impossible. She must have taken Valley Run at record speed, which means I have to as well if I'm going to ride with her up the lift that leads to the top of Eagle Mountain. I'm puffing when I ski up to the two skiers between the girl in the blue jacket and me, but a tap on the shoulder and a toss of my head sends them scurrying behind me. I don't often play the Eleanor Engebretsen card, but this is a special occasion, and I claim my place next to the mystery girl who isn't even breathing hard, though her cheeks are a sexy shade of red.

The ski lift carries the two people in front of us up, up, and away and we ski-shuffle onto the lift pad. She chooses the left and I go to the right. The chair hits the back of my knees and then I am sitting next to this girl, arms and hips and shoulders touching, and she's futzing with her goggles while I'm being swept away.

I should talk to her. I want to talk to her. I have a million questions to ask her, but my brain won't work. It's too busy trying to figure out how to steal sideways glances at her without getting busted. The first glance confirms what I suspected. No pro would be caught dead in rented skis and some off-brand jacket probably bought at Walmart. The second glance reveals a mess of auburn curls trying to escape a hand-knitted hat. The third glance gets me busted, but not until after I've checked out her long eyelashes dusted with snow, her full nibble-worthy lips, her slight overbite that makes her perfectly imperfect.

I was wrong.

So wrong.

This girl has all the right equipment.

"Hello, I'm up here." She looks at me until I pull my gaze off her body. A puff of smoke from her breath hits the freezing air and obscures her face for one second. Long enough for me to realize I like looking at her face. "I'm Kate Moreau."

"Ellie." I should say more, explain why I've been checking her out, but my brain has quit working.

"It's my first time at Lutsen. How about you?" Kate tries to rescue me from the awkward moment, but I hate small talk. Though I'm willing to listen to Kate's voice for hours, as long as I don't have to respond.

I stare through the V of my skis at the ski run and the tiny zooming skiers beneath us. I stare ahead at the gray-blue expanse of Lake Superior that begins at the foot of Lutsen and spreads across all of Minnesota's North Shore, ending who knows where. I stare at my knee, my boot, the clump of snow stuck to my ski—anything but the girl sitting next to me—and try to think of something clever to say.

"I asked if this is your first time at Lutsen, too." Kate looks at me, waiting for an answer I obviously should give her, but once again I'm rescued because the chairlift bounces to a stop and the bar lifts up. Kate quick steps it to the left while I stand there like an idiot and get my ass smacked before I realize I need to make a move.

"Uh, K-Kate?" My tongue, my fucking tongue. Such a traitor.

"Yeah?" She turns to look at me.

"It's my first time skiing Lutsen, too." I have no idea why I'm lying. No, that's another lie. I know perfectly well why I'm lying to Kate. Because I wish it was my first time. I'd give anything to start over.

"Cool. I'm heading to Mogen. Want to join me?" Kate asks and I notice her eyes for the first time. Gray streaked with slivers of pale blue. Little crinkles of skin around the corners. It makes me want to hear her laugh.

"Yeah, sure. Love to," I lie for the second time.

Mogen is Lutsen's terrain park. It's infested with snowboarders and peppered with deformed hills that insult real ski jumps. It's also Blair's favorite run and I can't think of Mogen without thinking of Blair. And I can't think of Blair. Not yet.

I am about to suggest another run, any other run, but Kate is a moving blur and, like on Freefall, she doesn't stop when she hits the top of Mogen. Someone really should tell her she's missing the best views, but that someone isn't going to be me.

I kick off and follow Kate. The run splits and she heads to the right toward a quarter-pipe jump. She slices through a swarm of snowboarders in a way that makes me proud to know her, even if it has only been for three whole minutes. I watch Kate approach the jump. I watch for the telltale signs that signals an amateur: A split second of hesitation. Surrendering to the reflex to pull back. Veering off at the last minute. But Kate does none of those as she takes the jump and somersaults through the air like she exists beyond the rules of gravity, and when she sticks a perfect landing, I forget how to breathe.

"That's what I'm talking about!" Kate fist pumps the air and whoops for joy, and then it's my turn to take her breath away. I shift my weight and aim straight for the quarter-pipe jump. My repertoire plays through my mind. A flatspin, an alley-oop, a twister? As usual, my body makes the decision for me. A Lincoln Loop it is. I bury my poles in my armpits and crouch low. The quarter-pipe rushes me and I feel it, the moment when my muscles take over. Wind slaps me across the face. My stomach presses against my spine. The sky tilts and then—

Images flood my mind.

A soft body, the ins and outs of which I know better than my own.

Laughing eyes. Lying eyes.

Long dark brown hair that bleeds blond. Ombré, she calls it. I should have known better than to fall for a girl who couldn't even be faithful to one hair color.

Blair. Blair. Goddamn Blair. Never meant for my heart. Impossible to forget.

My muscles contract. All of me contracts. The earth tilts on its axis. Fast and out of control, a wash of white. It's a different kind of fall, but like the others, it isn't free.

When the sparkling white starts to spin away, I spot Kate's face hovering above me and I pray to die right there at the foot of the quarter-pipe jump on Mogen.

"Oh my God, are you okay?" Kate asks.

I lie in the me-shaped indentation of snow, wriggling toes and bending wrists and trying to suck in air through lungs that have betrayed me as well. "Yeah, I think so."

Kate grabs my hand. "Let me help you up." She pulls me into a one-legged perch. I look for my other ski and spot it a few feet away, skewering a mogul. A sharp pain hits like a punch to the gut. I double over and grab my side. First Blair and now this—boffing a jump that on any other day would have been my bitch. The world wobbles again.

"Hey." Kate reaches out an arm and I grasp it like a kid in SkiWee holding onto the T-bar for dear life. "You sure you're okay?"

The pain begins to subside until I can straighten and look into her eyes. "Yeah, I'm fine. Sorry."

Her eyes crinkle at the corners. "For what? Falling? It happens." Kate yanks her hat off and a mop of wavy auburn hair tumbles around her face.

"Thanks for picking me up." Jesus! Did I say that? "From the ground, I mean. From the ground. You know, where you found me and…picked me up."

Kate laughs and I realize maybe Jack was right. She usually is when it comes to girls. Jack is my butch best friend whose real name is Lisa Marie, but she'll kick you in the balls if you call her that. Doesn't matter whether you have balls or not. She earned the nickname Jack when she came out, all at once and without giving a shit. Like that kid's toy, the one with the clown that couldn't take the pressure anymore and had to pop out of the damned box. That's Jack. Happy to be out, but always looking for the next box to pop into. Which, according to Jack, is precisely what I need to do to get over Blair.

Step one: Get a little tourist pussy. The sooner, the better.

Jack's words, not mine, and even though Jack can be crude, she's also brilliant as hell. She's got it all planned out—how I can get over my cheating girlfriend. She even named her master plan The Blair Bitch Project, but so far I've yet to find a tourist willing to sign up for some meaningless, heartbreak-erasing revenge sex. Still, Jack's plan is devious in a way that makes me sad she and I have zero chemistry, because I sure as hell love how her mind works.

I steal another glance at Kate. There's a sexy little glint in her eyes and a half smile on her face that could be interpreted as flirty. As Jack would say, no time like the present to get down with The Blair Bitch Project.

"How about I buy you a cocoa as a thank you?" Heat surges on my face until I'm certain I look like a friggin' stop sign. Round and red and telling Kate to stop, to not cross this lane.

Talk about a contradiction.

"I don't think so," Kate says and my stomach tightens. "But you could buy me a burger and fries to go with that cocoa."

"You got it."

Kate looks down the hill at my ski sticking out of the mogul. "Be right back." She skis over and yanks out my ski, then side steps her way back up Mogen. She drops the ski in front of me and I step into the binding. "You're lucky. You could have really hurt yourself."

It's subtle, but it's there. Kate's assumption that I couldn't handle the quarter-pipe jump, and it stings. So much I almost tell her I followed her down Freefall. That it was easy! That I'm Eleanor Engebretsen, *the* Eleanor Engebretsen, for crying out loud, and that I'm only off balance because my ex-girlfriend sent the wrong lover a text. But instinct tells me to shut the fuck up, so I do.

Kate surveys the slope and shakes her head. "We're going to take it slow and skip the rest of the jumps. If you get in trouble, for God's sake, sit your ass down and yell for help. Got it?"

"Yeah." My ego takes a hit, but my libido surges. "I got it."

"Okay, then. Follow me." And she's off.

One quick dart toward the moguls would clarify things once and for all, and yeah, it's tempting. But then Kate looks back at me, and it strikes me that following this girl might lead me exactly where I want to go.

As promised, Kate takes it slow, hugging the curves of the hill in a way that makes me see more than just her body. I see her form, the way she uses the slope and the pull of the hill to her advantage. The way she reacts without thought or fear. Three minutes down the hill, I'm pretty sure Kate's talent is more born than trained. Five minutes down, I'm certain it doesn't matter.

"We made it!" Kate says when we reach Rosie's Chalet. She's too polite to say what she really means—that *I* made it, miracle of miracles. She slides her rented skis into the rack and smiles at me.

"Thanks to you." I lay it on thick as I slide my Rossignols next to Kate's skis. "C'mon. You've earned that burger and fries."

"Don't forget the cocoa." Kate grins as she takes off her gloves and shoves them in her pockets.

"Absolutely not," I promise her.

We walk toward Rosie's, where cocoa is going to be served, hopefully with a heavy sprinkling of sweet talk. Kate holds the door for me and I walk forward, my attention momentarily drawn to her long fingers circled with silver rings and her neatly trimmed nails.

It's impossible to stop my imagination from fast-forwarding as we step into the women's locker room to ditch our jackets and clunky ski boots. I sit on a bench and bend over to unclamp my buckles. It's the perfect vantage point to steal more glances at Kate as she unzips her jacket, but she catches me and smiles a Mona Lisa smile. Indecipherable. Infuriating. My stocking feet hit the floor and soak up the snow that has dripped in clumps from my boots and turned to puddles. I shiver.

"What's wrong?" Kate asks me.

"Nothing." I tell her. "Just cold feet. I'll warm up soon enough."

She laughs like she's reading between all my stupid lines. I put on my tennis shoes and lead Kate upstairs to Rosie's. Of course, getting her on my turf is only the first part of my plan. The next part depends on whether or not Jack is working the front desk at Eagle Ridge Lodge. She'd better be. Otherwise The Blair Bitch Project is dead in the water before I can give Kate a reason to take off all those rings.

CHAPTER TWO

Rosie's Chalet looks like it's been attacked by elves high on peppermint-flavored crack. Seriously. I hate how businesses along the North Shore pander to the tourists, especially at Christmas. We cut down evergreens, screw them, and stick them in corners. As if that weren't enough humiliation, we throw fake lights and cheesy ornaments on them. Puke. Evergreens belong outside. They don't deserve to die so some idiot can sing "O Tannenbaum" while staring at dried-up needles clinging to dead branches, but no one's asked my opinion on the subject of holiday décor so far.

Kate and I head upstairs to the cafeteria where hamburgers and fries are served with an abundance of grease. Someone has woven tinsel through every antler chandelier. Probably Grandma, who, according to the DJ over the sound system, got run over by a reindeer. It's Sunday, which means the Christmas ski weekend is almost over, thank God. There's hardly an overpriced Dale of Norway sweater in sight since most of the tourists have headed home in time for school to resume tomorrow, though there is a healthy scattering of locals. Like me, they prefer to ski when the resort is practically deserted. And like me, they know the booth by the stone fireplace is reserved for the once Olympic almost hero Peder Engebretsen and his daughter, the rising star. But that's not where I guide Kate. Confused stares follow me, but I don't care. The Blair Bitch Project is all about doing whatever it takes, whoever it takes, to mend a broken heart, so I sure as hell am not going to let Kate anywhere near the photos of Dad taken in 1988 in Calgary, pre-disaster, not to mention the pictures of me jumping at Big Sur and Whistler and Iron Mountain.

For The Blair Bitch Project to work, I need to be Ellie, the out of her league skier Kate rescued from fractured limbs or certain death on Mogen. How else am I going to get Kate to take the short leap from compassion to passion?

I choose the booth farthest from The Engebretsen Pictorial Hall of Fame, which is also the one nearest the kitchen where the scent of ketchup and diced onions and garlic bread hangs heavy in the air. We slide into the booth and sit across from each other. Kate grins at me and time feels like it stops. I lose myself in her eyes, her gray-blue eyes, but then she looks away from me and toward the cafeteria line. "You did say something about a burger and fries, didn't you?"

"Right. And cocoa." I climb out of the booth.

"With lots and lots of whipped cream," Kate says.

I nod and head toward the cafeteria, bumping against protruding chairs and stumbling over duffel bags as the image of Kate wearing nothing but whipped cream fills my mind. The cafeteria line is long, and I use the time to try to answer the same old questions. *Is she? Or isn't she? And does she know I am?*

It isn't the suspense that gets me. It's the possibility I'm making a fool of myself that pisses me off. I grab burgers and fries and top two mugs of cocoa with a scandalous amount of whipped cream, but I still don't have the first clue if my ski buddy is a potential fuck buddy. Frankly, I need Jack with all her smooth moves. She scores like nobody I know. Me? Once I'm in the game, I'm fine. It's the prelim qualifiers that kill me.

I return to the booth and set the food and cocoa in front of Kate.

She lifts the mug to her mouth. "Mm," she says, sipping the sweet hot cocoa, and when she sets the mug down on the table I can't help but stare at the bit of whipped cream clinging to her upper lip. Flick. That damn tongue. How am I supposed to come up with any words, much less the perfect words, when Kate is flicking her tongue at me?

I am about to give up and ask Kate to hand over her queer card when the sound of laughter from the direction of the fireplace grabs me by the guts and twists me inside out. I turn to look, like I could resist, and sure enough. There's Geoffrey-with-a-*G* and Blair in all her pink and white snow bunny glory sitting at my table. Laughing. Holding hands. Perfecting the art of prefuck flirting.

"Bastards."

Kate follows my gaze and fixes her eyes on the guy across from Blair.

"Your ex?" she asks.

It registers that Kate is referring to Geoffrey-with-a-*G*, the sole heir of Lutsen's richest family who stole Blair from me by offering her the one thing I didn't already possess and couldn't strap on.

Money. Loads of it.

"No," I say. "Just someone who reminds me of my ex back home." I force my eyes away from Blair to Kate.

"Where's home?" Kate asks.

Sometimes, when I'm lucky, lies come to me like muscle memory, effortlessly and without the need to think. "Minneapolis. You?"

Kate takes another sip of cocoa. "Tahoe."

"As in Nevada? What the hell are you doing up here?" I forget about Blair and Geoffrey for a second. One glorious second.

"Mom came to check on a business opportunity and I tagged along for the skiing." Kate takes a bite of her hamburger. "What brings you to Lutsen?"

"Christmas weekend ski vacation with my folks." I drum my fingers on the table and try to figure a way out of what is quickly becoming the unsexiest conversation ever.

Blair laughs from across the room. Loud and high and not at all like the sound of Blair laughing I've come to know so well this past year. My guts twist again and I cringe. I can't help it.

Kate reaches for a napkin and her hand brushes mine for a moment. I look up and find her eyes trained on me. "I'm sorry," she says.

"Don't be. I'm over her." *Her*, I say and swallow hard. "The girl from back home, that is. My ex."

And I thought flying off a ski jump at sixty miles per hour took guts.

Kate's eyes widen like she's taken it all in. Blair and Geoffrey and me. "But you're over her?" she asks. "The girl back home who looks like the pretty girl over there?"

"Absolutely. I couldn't be more over her." I've never lied so much in my life. It's so easy. And right now it sure as hell feels better than the truth.

"I'm glad." Kate looks me straight in the eyes.

I pick up my hamburger, but I feel bloated with lies. Like I can't stomach one more thing so I put the hamburger down on my plate, but not before Kate notices.

"Aren't you hungry?"

And then I spy it, the inrun to the jump I need to take. "Starving," I say. "But not for food." It feels too brazen, too sudden, and a flush of heat crawls up my neck, but a half smile plays at the corner of Kate's mouth.

"You're not thirsty either." Kate glances at my untouched mug.

Girl doesn't miss a thing.

"I'm in the mood for something with a little more kick." I feel myself soaring through the air.

Kate raises an eyebrow. "Too bad they don't serve alcohol to minors at Rosie's."

The entire chalet fades out of focus. Even the table by the fireplace. "Yeah, too bad."

Gravity has me in its grip and is pulling me, down and down and down toward the landing strip where maybe, just maybe, Kate is waiting for me. "My parents are going to be skiing for hours. I don't suppose you'd want to raid the minibar in my room?"

Kate taps the silver ring on her index finger against the side of her cocoa mug and smiles.

❖

I walk with Kate, head high, through the cafeteria and past the table by the fireplace. We grab our coats in the locker room and step outside into the brisk late-afternoon air. It's a short walk from Rosie's to Eagle Ridge Resort, but it feels like miles. We walk past Papa Charlie's where the thump of music is only slightly softer than the creaking of gondolas overhead on their cables as they carry skiers to Summit Chalet. For once luck is with me and Jack is working the front desk, grinning like mad at the sight of me with Anyone Other Than Blair.

I do a quick self pat down and try to look confused. "Sorry." I approach the counter. "I think I lost my key card on the slopes. Could you give me another?"

Jack runs a hand across her cropped black hair, performs a full body scan of Kate, and grins at me. "That was condo 103, the suite with the Jacuzzi, right?" she asks.

"Right," I say.

Jack punches a few numbers into the computer and holds out a key card to me. Her latest tattoo crawls up her hand.

Lean in to your...

The last word disappears beneath the cuff of Jack's uniform shirt, but I don't need to see it to complete the phrase.

Death. It's what my father teaches every member of his ski jumping team, the Lab Rats.

I take the key card and grin at Jack. "Thanks."

"No prob. Have fun." Jack winks and I could kill her.

The first difference between Blair and Kate becomes evident as we walk the short distance toward condo 103. Blair chatters. Endlessly. Like it's her personal crusade to kill all silence, all suspense, all surprise.

Kate walks quietly, her hand swinging by her side and brushing up against mine often enough to make me wonder. Not often enough to make me know.

We reach the condo and I slide the card into the keypad. The light turns green and my hand closes on the handle. I am about to pull the door open when Kate's hand closes on mine. It's a question and I answer it by letting my thumb run across her finger and over the delicate design of her ring. Kate lets go and I pull open the door. Together we step into the room and let the door close behind us.

As usual, Kate doesn't wait to take in the view. "That line about the minibar was bullshit, right?"

I nod and say nothing.

Neither of us reaches for the light. I stare at the dark shadows that outline the bed, at Kate in the mirror above the Jacuzzi as she turns toward me. As her arm slips behind my back. As her hand reaches for my face.

It's like a dream or a TV show, watching Kate move in the mirror, but the illusion shatters because then the real Kate is in my arms—her mouth on mine, her hand on my breast over my clothes, and everything becomes far too real.

I pull away and Kate crosses the room to stand beside the bed.

"After you," I tell her, obeying the stronger of the two needs at war within me.

Lead.

Or be led.

Kate unbuttons her flannel shirt and stands in front of me, silently, in a gray tank top. She stands there and lets me take in the exactness of her: broad shoulders, lean arm muscles.

Kate does not blink when she looks at me. "Now you. One of us takes something off. Then the other. Deal?"

The other need, the one that is hot and located between my legs, makes the decision for me. "Deal."

I reach for the hem of my shirt and pull it over my head. It shifts my sports bra and the air, when it hits, is as shocking as the position I'm in. I drop my shirt at my feet and yank my bra back in place.

This girl gets nothing from me for free.

"Your turn." I stare at her.

Kate laughs, slips off one ring, and lays it on the bedside table.

"The fuck?" I take a step forward, but Kate stops me with two words.

"Your turn."

I glance at the remaining rings on her fingers and sigh.

I take off my shoes.

Kate slips off a second ring.

I fumble with buttons and zippers but eventually my pants drop to the floor and I step out of them and stand there in nothing but socks, cotton underwear, and a sports bra.

A third ring joins the first two on the nightstand.

This girl is going to be the death of me.

Finally, when I am in nothing but my underwear and one sock, Kate pulls off her tank top. When I am barefoot, she sheds her pants.

And that's when I discover another difference between Blair and Kate.

Blair is all Victoria's Secret push-up bras and lace thongs— the perfect fuckable angel. Or so I always thought.

Until Kate stands in front of me in nothing but a pair of men's jockey shorts. Who is this girl? What have I gotten myself into?

Kate sits on the bed. I move to sit beside her, but she loops her arm around my back and pulls me onto her lap until we are tits to tits, and I discover the biggest difference of all between Kate and Blair, the one that makes me unlearn everything I thought I knew.

Kate puts her hand on the inside of my thigh above my knee. I hold my breath while she slides her hand up my leg.

"Breathe," she tells me as she presses her mouth over the dip at the base of my neck, her tongue hot and wet on my skin. Her hand moves closer. And then closer. "Ellie, breathe," she says again and I do.

In shallow, trembling breaths that leave my head spinning, I stare at her hand as it inches closer until her fingers brush against the elastic edge of my underwear and every part of me freezes. My legs, my arms, my lungs.

"It's okay," Kate whispers into my neck. "I've got you."

The freezing melts into trembling.

Her fingers flick over damp fabric and I gulp in a deep breath.

"Ellie?" she pulls back and looks at me, the unasked question written on her face.

I nod. She slips her finger between cotton and skin.

Kate keeps her eyes on me as she delves between, then in, while the war of the dueling needs rages within me, stronger than ever.

Lead.

Or be led.

Her free hand reaches for my breast. My muscles contract. All of me contracts. The earth tilts on its axis.

This is all wrong! I want to shout as she pinches my nipple. *I give. You take. You're supposed to lie there and chatter away until I make it impossible for you to speak. That's how I know I'm any good at this. Don't you know that?*

Kate, I discover, does not know that, and the words don't come—though I do. Fast and out of control, in a wash of white, I come and I come and I come until I collapse against Kate, my head on her shoulder, sweat dripping between my breasts, and without a single thought of Blair.

When the sparkling white starts to spin away I open my eyes, brush away the beginning of a tear on my face, and pray to die right there in her arms.

CHAPTER THREE

L ater, much later, Kate and I leave condo 103 with the minibar, the Jacuzzi, and me fully drained. Even so, I'm not ready for our night together to be over. There's the small matter of turning my world right side up by going down on Kate, but her cell phone has been pinging texts for the last hour and Kate's mom is past accepting excuses. It sucks, but there's not a damn thing I can do about it so I walk Kate back to the lobby of Eagle Ridge where a smirking Jack watches my every move from behind the front desk. Jack, I ignore. The awkward silence that opens up between Kate and me? I wish I could.

I shift my weight from my left foot to my right. Back to my left. Jack coughs. Kate grins. I slide my eyes to the glass door behind Kate that leads to the parking lot and stare at my reflection.

Some Twilight Zone version of Eleanor Engebretsen stares back at me, messed up inside and out, and Jesus fucking Christ, I don't recognize myself. Who is that girl? The one who got dumped for some guy? The one who let some other girl tit-tickle her into submission? No fucking clue.

Kate's pocket pings angrily again and she pulls out her cellphone and scans the text. "I really gotta go, Ellie," she says.

I look at Kate. At her mussed-up hair. At her slight overbite. At the laugh lines around her gray-blue eyes. It isn't like I'm unaware I'm botching the chance of a lifetime here. Another round with

Kate is probably mine for the asking. Maybe two if I'm lucky and she's in town for a few days. Fuck. The old me, the pre-Blair me, would have been all over that shit.

Kate reaches for the door handle and my stomach flip-flops. I can practically hear Jack screaming in my mind, but the words will not come.

"I had fun," Kate says.

I nod. Pathetic. Trust me, I know.

"'Bye, Ellie." Kate smiles and then she pulls open the door and walks out of my life. I watch her high step through the snowy sidewalk, growing smaller and fainter as she recedes into the darkness. My head pounds. My chest tightens. My voice pushes its way up my throat and out of my mouth.

"Wait!" I try to shout, but it comes out like a squeak. Not that it matters. Kate is too far away to hear me.

It takes Jack about .002 seconds to abandon the front desk and rush me. "What the fuck was that?" She stares at me. "Since when do you choke?"

The BFF code according to Jack demands I spill my truth and so I do. "Since now, I guess."

Jack's eyes dart to Kate who has reached the parking lot. She takes a step toward the door and something inside me snaps.

"Oh no, you don't." I block Jack, which may be the stupidest thing I've done all night. Jack, I know, could snap me in two without working up a sweat.

"Say her name," Jack plants her hands on her wide hips.

"Kate," I say.

"*Mmmbeeep.* Play again."

I know perfectly well what name Jack wants me to say. But I can't yet. It still cuts too deep on the way out.

"This is for your own good, El." Either Jack's reactions have gotten quicker or mine have gotten slower because she steps past me easily and yanks the glass door open. Horrified, I watch her sprint down the sidewalk and rush Kate in the parking lot. She must have hollered something because Kate stops and turns to look at Jack. And then Jack is talking and big Italian gesturing toward the lobby where I'm silently wishing a plague of ingrown pubic hair on my best friend.

Kate nods. Seems to say something. My imagination goes wild, but then Jack digs into her pocket and pulls out a little piece of paper and a pen. Kate scribbles something on the paper. It's all horrible and awful, and I take vow after vow after vow to make anyone my new best friend. Even Geoffrey-with-a-*G*. Okay, maybe not him, but anyone else. Then Jack is stepping aside and Kate is climbing into her car and Jack is sprinting back to me, grinning like she broke the Olympic record for babe scoring, and I'm deciding if I'm going to punch her or kick her or both. Jack blows into the lobby with a gust of winter wind, but even that can't cool me down.

"What the fuck do you think you were doing?" I clench my fists and glare, but Jack, unconcerned, slowly unfolds the piece of paper in her hands.

"My job, El. Surprisingly, I actually did my job. Did you know Eagle Ridge Resort rewards employees for every satisfaction survey they get filled out? They do. I get two per shift and there's a ten-dollar bonus on my paycheck. Plus, it's a good deal. Guests answer a few questions and in return we send them discounts to lure them back. Of course, they have to give us their full name, address, email, and phone number." Jack kickstands her leg behind her and leans against the wall. "By the way, she rated her overall satisfaction seven out of ten." She grins as she holds out the piece of paper to me. "I'm disappointed, El. I always thought you'd score at least an eight."

"Thanks, I think." I take the survey and step into the freezing night air, letting the door slam shut on the sound of Jack belly laughing. Ahead of me lies the parking lot and my car and the road that leads to home and my real life.

Such as it is.

❖

"Eleanor?" My father's voice sneaks through my closed bedroom door and interrupts a perfectly fine dream of long fingers and no rings.

"Stay," I tell Kate as I hold on to the dream of her as long as I can. I should have said please because she slips away, slowly and then all at once, and I awaken to find myself lying in bed in the me-shaped indentation that has somehow grown too big or shrunk too small during the night.

I crack open my eyes to spot Blair smiling at me from the framed picture on my nightstand and, next to her, the unopened Christmas gift I bought her, a pair of one-carat diamond earrings paid for with money saved up from years of birthday and Christmas gifts, all cash and all earmarked for my future expenses as an Olympian. Considering her Christmas gift for me, the one I opened even though it wasn't meant for my eyes, I feel like a total schmuck. The Eagle Ridge survey lies on the nightstand next to Blair's picture and present. For a moment I wonder how Blair would have rated her satisfaction with me. Lower than a seven, I'd bet. Why else would she have left me for some dick?

I wriggle my toes and bend my wrists and try to find something that feels normal. Light crawls down the wall and falls like snow on the knotty-pine floor of my bedroom like it has every other morning of my life so far, but even that doesn't feel normal.

Nothing has since Mom left.

I sit on the edge of my bed and pull my comforter around my shoulders. Cold creeps up from the floor and penetrates me. I take a deep breath and feel it: the mourning in this morning.

And then I hear it: one note, long and wailing. It attaches, one to another, until the string of notes transform into a song that morphs into an image that pushes into my mind. A woman. My mother. An older version of me. Standing in front of the living room window: golden head bent, ice blue eyes closed, body swaying, chin and violin fused, arm slowly pulling her truth from the delicate strings.

Until the day she found a truer truth.

We'll talk on the phone every day, I promise. We can Skype. You can visit. Boston's not so far away. Don't look at me like that, El. It's the Philharmonic, for God's sake. This is my *dream. Do you hear me? My dream.*

Yeah, yeah, I hear you. But only because Dad plays that stupid CD with your solo every damn morning. Closest thing I've gotten yet to daily chats.

"Eleanor, you up yet?" Dad's voice breaks on the last word and the hot prickling crawls through me until I want to shout at him. *She's gone, Dad. Gone.* G-O-N-E. *And she's never coming back. Get over it.*

But I don't. Instead, I pick up the survey and open it. One phone call. That's all it would take and I could lose myself in Kate's arms again, but that's the problem. Engebretsens aren't allowed to lose. Ever. I put the piece of paper back on my nightstand and reach for the picture frame. Blair. Almost as beautiful as the future I imagined for us with me at PyeongChang, competing against the best, while Blair, in the stands, obnoxiously announces to everyone within earshot that her girl, Ellie Engebretsen, would be bringing home the gold. The back slides off easily and I hold her in my hands once more. What happened to that picture-perfect future? Was Blair always this shallow? This paper-thin? The prickling heat comes again and I grip the edges of the picture until they bend. It feels good and so I tear off a corner. And another. Until the whole of her lying, smiling face has been turned to confetti. Why should I be the only one shredded?

"Eleanor! Get out of bed now!" Dad switches into coach voice.

"Yeah, yeah. I'm up." I stand and the bits of Blair flutter to the floor. "What's the temp outside?" It's a stupid question. Cold is cold is cold.

"Negative three. Wind chill of twenty-five below."

"Fuck." I take a deep breath and reach for the wicking shirt that lies crumpled on my floor. I follow with heavyweight fleece, a shell jacket, wool socks, and a pair of ski pants. The layers can't protect me from all the harsh elements I face, but they do keep me warm. When I'm properly layered, I walk to my window and hold back the white curtain. Not one flake of snow has fallen overnight to soften the spaces and places of my life. The parking lot. The roof of the equipment shed. The jump and the landing zone. Even the great lake in the distance—all are bare and exposed, protected only by a sheet of hard ice. A few miles south of me, skiers are breaking the crust on Lutsen Mountain's snow bed. A few miles north of me, Lutsen locals are sprinkling salt on sidewalks. I've spent my life here, somewhere between town and mountain, wishing for a fresh dusting of snow. It can't soften all the hard things, but sometimes it cushions the fall.

I let go of the curtain and my silly wishes. It's time to get on with my day.

There is no Christmas tree in our living room. No stupid elves sitting on shelves. No blinking lights or lit candles or packages wrapped in gaudy paper, and I'm fine with all that. Though I almost miss the diabetic-coma-inducing Christmas music when I find Tchaikovsky's concerto, the second movement, looping obnoxiously. I hit the stop button on the sound system and in the silence that follows I hear Dad in the kitchen, assembling my breakfast.

That's right, assembling. What he's doing cannot be called cooking.

I swing open the door and spot Dad dropping raw eggs into the blender. One, two, three, I count them as I plant my tired ass on a stool at the kitchen counter and groan. Loudly.

"What happened to the music?" Dad asks as he shovels a heaping scoop of protein powder along with a liberal glurg of fish oil and a sprinkling of flaxseed into the blender. "I was listening to that."

"It's not healthy for you," I tell him and prop my head on my hand, changing the subject back to something safe. "And what the fuck is wrong with a bowl of Wheaties? I thought they were supposed to be the breakfast of champions."

"It's not healthy for you." He grins and hits the puree button on the blender. "Drink more." He pours the green goo into a glass and shoves it toward me. "Swear less."

"Mm." I take a sip and screw up my face. "Fucking delicious."

Dad, I figure, needs at least one person he can count on.

After I've chugged the breakfast of chumpions, I follow Dad downstairs to Gravity Lab, Dad's ski school and pro shop. Unlike our apartment, which looks like it's decorated with garage sale leftovers since Mom took everything she wanted with her, Gravity Lab offers the most carefully curated pro shop east of the Rockies. Thermodynamic clothing, action cams that mount on helmets, custom made skis—you name it, we've got it, which is plain smart business. Selling weekend skiers the kind of equipment that makes them feel like pros is a good way to fund my travel expenses to Continental and World Cup competitions. It also draws locals who are willing to pay tuition fees to be one of the Lab Rats, Dad's elite ski jumping team.

Of course, while the rest of the Lab Rats are eating breakfast burritos and heading back to Lutsen High now that winter break is over, I get to spend my day following Dad's meticulous training program, a grueling combination of weight lifting, plyometrics, cardio, and jump training. I'd love to go to school, too, but not Lutsen High. For years I've been begging Dad to enroll me in the Winter Sports School, a high school that runs from April to November, which frees up the winter months for athletic training and competition. Unfortunately the Winter Sports School is in Utah and Dad built Gravity Lab in Minnesota so I'm pretty much stuck taking private lessons with a tutor during the summer. It's not ideal, but it has kept the board of education off our asses for the last three years, and after this summer I'll graduate. At least I won't have to wear a stupid gown or a square hat or a tassel.

Another so-called perk in the life of an Olympic hopeful.

By three p.m., I'm perched on the start bar ninety meters above the ground, skis strapped to my feet, and watching car after car pull into the parking lot in front of Gravity Lab. The pain in my side is sharp. My lungs feel shriveled in my chest, like they've given up hope of ever breathing warm air again. The muscles in my legs would go on strike if they had the strength to walk a picket line. This is my seventh and last jump before Lab Rat practice and the only thing keeping me going is the hope that Blair and Geoffrey have had the good sense to drop the team.

"C'mon, Eleanor." Dad's voice slices through the cold air. "Time to get a move on!"

Below me he stands on the coach's stand parallel to the takeoff point, megaphone in one hand and cane in the other. Jack, at the bottom of the hill, has arrived early enough to watch my last jump.

Twenty-five below zero wind sinks its teeth into my exposed skin. Icy fingers scratch through every one of my protective layers. The tingling of fear—the true inrun to any jump—starts in my belly and spreads through my body.

"Make me proud!" Dad yells up to me.

It's not a request. It never was.

PART II: TAKEOFF

If I've heard Dad preach it once to the Lab Rats, I've heard him say it a million times.

Take off like you're ending a bad relationship.

And he should know.

Step 1: Don't create unnecessary friction.

In other words, don't let the skis brush the side of the tracks during the inrun. It's a stupid way to lose speed.

Step 2: Break up. Don't be broken up with.

Wait too long and a jumper can find herself trying to launch off nothing but air. Take off while there's still something solid under your feet. Seems like that's one bit of advice I should have taken from Dad.

Step 3: Lean in to your death.

Everything dies eventually. Airtime. Blair time. And Dad is right—the difference between losers and winners is simple. Losers pull back from the terror of takeoff. Or maybe they're weighed down by grief that the run has ended. Winners lean toward their deaths, free of fear, and live to fly again.

I am a winner. I do what I was trained to do.

But not until I breathe.

In and out. In and out. One hand on my stomach over the bodysuit I wear. One hand pressed against my helmet. Not much in the way of protection, all things considered.

In and out, in and out, I breathe. Until they peel off and float away, the faces I wear. Blair's betrayed. Kate's one-night stand. Mom's abandoned child. Dad's last shot at gold. They float away on the exhalation of breath. Already I feel lighter. It's tempting to rush toward takeoff, but still it tugs at me, the weight of the heaviest thing I need to shed.

The instinct to live another day.

Trust me, jumping with baggage like that is no way to fly, though it is a good way to die.

I trace the tracks of the inrun with my eyes and imagine what is to come. My calves and thigh muscles stretching as I crouch low and center myself. My core driving me forward. The steep slope of the inrun and the momentum I've created to hurtle me, cheeks flapping against the wind, into the unknown.

My breath drags in deep and pushes out hard. Bits of spit come with it, but I don't care. There's no one around to impress.

In and out, I breathe. In and out. Five counts in. Seven counts out. The start bar grows warm beneath my ass and that won't do.

His voice blasts through the megaphone. "Sometime today, Eleanor?"

It comes to me, finally, the sharp edge I need. Without mercy and cutting deep, it carves into me until I am hollow even to my bones and ready to fly.

I stand, crouch low, and then I am speeding down the inrun—thirty miles per hour, forty, fifty, sixty. Adrenaline floods my body, arming me the way a bullet arms a gun. The way a thumb cocks a hammer. The way a finger pulls a trigger. Until I explode into the space between heaven and the hard ground below.

Takeoff.

CHAPTER FOUR

Time slows. Stops.
Thinking slows. Stops.
My body takes over. I spread my skis into a V in front of me and lean forward. Far, far forward. Beyond the edge of sanity and yeah, I'm not gonna lie, it's scary as hell. Standard ski jumping equipment should include a pair of wings. Sure would help with the flying part and they might come in handy in the event a jumper lands at the pearly gates.

I reach out with my arms and hold them parallel to my body. They're not quite wings, but they give me some stabilization as I fly. I've taught my upper body to stay loose in case the wind changes.

And the wind always changes.

I shift a little to my right to correct my course. My eyes stare down the knoll of the hill to the K Point, the line that marks the average par or achieved distance on the particular jump. In ski jumping, all the difficult math is saved for calculating flight formation angles to achieve maximum aerodynamic lift. The actual scoring part is simple. Land on the K Point on a normal hill, which is ninety meters, and score sixty points. Land behind the K Point and lose two distance points for every meter. Land ahead of it and gain two distance points for every meter. Distance points are straightforward. Style points, not so much. Each jumper faces five judges who award up to twenty points for style, and they examine everything. How smooth the skis are during the jump, how well the skier is balanced, overall form, and whether the jumper nails a telemark-style landing. The top and bottom scores are thrown out, so sixty is the max a jumper can get for style points. It all sounds easy, but it's hard as fuck.

I fly with the shifting wind and merge into it. Two seconds. Three. Four. I stop counting because the wind has ceased to be wind and has become my breath. I am no longer Eleanor Engebretsen. Or Ellie. Or even El. I am no longer seventeen, or made of flesh and bone, or ruled by my head or heart. I am me. Nameless and uncontainable and free.

Of course, it has to end. Nothing this good lasts forever. Bit by bit, I descend toward the ground and pull my body back in preparation for landing. I spread my arms and bend my knees as I move one ski in front of the other. It has come to this. From inrun to takeoff to flight time to this moment. The things that can go wrong during a landing are incalculable. Over- or undercorrecting body rotation. An unbalanced distribution of weight. Hell, even a clump of the snow. Any number of factors can turn nirvana into nightmare in no time at all and I've lost count of the times I've wound up looking like roadkill in the outrun.

But not this time.

This time the magic happens. One ski and then another, I touch down with a fluidity that tells me I nailed full points for style.

"Fuck yeah!" I drop my arms by my side and ski toward Jack at the bottom of the hill. I cut deep into the snow as I approach her and send up a sheet of slush and ice. It's a cocky move, but I've earned it.

"That was awesome!" Jack runs a hand across her face. Bits of snow cling to her mitten. "Hope you're packed and ready for the Olympics, El."

But it's not Jack's opinion that matters. I look at my father, tougher than the toughest jump. Harder than the hardest fall. He limps down the ramp from the coach's stand, cane in one hand and megaphone in the other, and aims straight for Gravity Lab.

"Well?" I yell at him.

"Good." He leans heavily on his cane, plunging it deep into the snow. He yanks it out, gives it a shake, and continues to walk away without glancing at me.

"Just good?" I throw my words at him the way I'd like to throw my skis or icicles or daggers. At his back.

"Yep. Just good." He leaves a trail of two footprints and one small cane-sized circle in the snow behind him.

"Hey, Mr. Engebretsen," Jack yells. "The eye doctor called. Your appointment for your vision check is scheduled for tomorrow morning. Don't be late."

I can't hear the sound of his laughter, but I'm pretty sure I see his shoulders move up and down as he walks toward the Lab Rats who await his brilliance.

"Thanks," I tell Jack. There's sympathy in her smile, but there's something else in her eyes. A warning. "What?"

Jack looks at the ground. Kicks the snow. "They're here, El. I can't believe they had the nerve to show up, but they did."

She doesn't need to tell me who.

I look toward Gravity Lab where Blair and her boy toy are most likely inside the gym, working out. It's ridiculously easy and painful to picture. Blair poised on an eighteen-inch block, Geoffrey-with-a-*G* in front of her, his hands on her hips. Touching her. *Touching her!* Blair crouching. Leaping. Like she's a tiger wearing the body of a girl. Like she's known it all along. Springing into the air, trusting him not to let her fall the way she trusted me once. The image in my mind is toxic enough to kill even the strongest dream. If Blair isn't going to be cheering me on at PyeongChang, maybe I don't want it anymore.

"Fuck that shit." I bend over, sever the bindings between the heel of my boots and my skis, and step out of the restraints that hold me. "I quit." I stand and face Jack.

"Quit what?" Jack blinks. Again. Looks at me like I'm a stranger to her.

"All of it." The rightness of my decision swells inside me. "The Lab Rats. Ski jumping. This whole fucked-up existence I call life."

"To do what?" she asks, her glare hot enough to melt my jumpsuit and leave me standing there, even more naked and vulnerable than I am. "Sew Halloween costumes for dogs and sell them at local pet stores? Become a juggler and make your living off street performances in Duluth? 'Cuz that's a wonderful way to use your God-given gifts, El. Brilliant."

"Bitch." I glare right back at her.

"Fine. I'm a bitch." Jack does not back down. Jack never backs down. "I'm also your best friend. Way I see it, it's not my job to stamp the invitations to your pity party."

I flinch.

"It *is* my job to help you pull off The Blair Bitch Project."

I picture Blair, sure and steady midair on Geoffrey's hands. My Blair, my girl, the bitch who leapt into his arms like it was the easiest thing in the world.

"What do you want to do, El?" Jack asks the question that trumps all other questions. "Sulk? Or strike back?"

❖

The exercise room inside Gravity Lab always smells like sweat. Doesn't matter how often we air it out, what type of disinfectant we use, how much we bleach the equipment, the room smells like sweat, but that's never bothered me until I walk in and spot Dad, clipboard in hand, coaching Blair and Geoffrey on imitation jumps.

The good pure scent of sweat changes. Like it's been corrupted by something stronger. Nastier.

"Nice job, Blair. Beautiful balance. Now relax your hips. That's right. And again."

Geoffrey lowers Blair gently onto the block where she crouches and springs toward him like she can't wait to get his hands on her body.

"Keep up the good work, you two." Dad walks past them. They're not the only two people in the room, but it feels that way. The girl I thought I could trust and the guy I once considered a friend. Also known as the girl who rejected me and the guy she rejected me for. Maybe not everyone in the room feels like tossed-away garbage in their presence, but I do. I sure as fuck do.

"Strike back," I whisper to Jack. "I want to strike back."

"Now you're talking." Jack leads me to the station across from Blair and Geoffrey. I step onto the block and find myself staring at Geoffrey-with-a-*G* and his obscenely large biceps that hold Blair above his head. Next to him, Blair looks tiny. Like a gust of wind could snatch her from his hands and carry her away.

He places her back on the block and suddenly we are facing one another, Blair and I, for the first time since the last time, when she couldn't bring herself to look me in the eyes.

She still can't and it would be almost funny, the way her eyes rove around the room until her gaze settles on Jack's ass, if it didn't hurt so damn much that even her eyes are off limits to me. To people not in the know, it probably looks like Blair hasn't given up girls for good. Not by a long shot. But Blair knows and I know, the deep red that spreads across her face has nothing to do with Jack's glutes and everything to do with her guilt.

Blair crouches and leaps, but not before her eyes flicker toward me for a second. Not even a full second. And then she's back in Geoffrey's hands, beyond my reach.

Jack clears her throat and grabs my hips. "So, tell me, El. Who was that hot chick I saw you with last night?"

"W-what? Who—?"

I don't remember fat twisting being part of imitation jumps, but Jack is making up new rules as she goes.

"That hot chick you nailed last night. What was her name?" Jack twists again to make sure she has my full attention.

"You mean Kate?" A surge of power hits me when I say her name.

Blair's head jerks toward us. Her body follows and it isn't pretty. Arms flap. Legs flail. Geoffrey-with-a-*G* panics and tries to widen his stance for stability. Above him, Blair's body tilts over Geoffrey's center of gravity.

"Don't you dare!" Blair's voice tumbles from above and then the rest of her follows. Through the air, toward the floor, Blair falls as Geoffrey scrambles, trying like hell to catch her by grabbing arms, ass, boobs, hair, whatever he can. It's a grotesque grope session for everyone to see.

Blair lands with a thud and a whimper on the floor. The look she sends Geoffrey-with-a-*G* says his dick and right hand are going to be best friends for a long time to come.

"El, you are the luckiest bastard I know," Jack says.

I savor the moment as I crouch and leap into the air. Jack's arms are concrete beams. Steel girders. They hold me firm while I look down at the crumpled mess on the floor that was once my girlfriend. Jack lowers me onto the block when I've had my fill, and God, does it feel good to stand on my own again.

"Tell me you had her screaming your name before the night was over." Jack throws a grin in Blair's general direction. Casual-like, as only Jack can.

Me? I'm happy to play along. "You know I never fuck and tell, Jack."

Too much? Too far?

Not by the wonderful awful look on Blair's face.

CHAPTER FIVE

Dad cuts practice short and calls for a Lab Rat meeting, which is fine with my screaming ass muscles. I settle down on the mat next to Jack and as far away from Blair and Geoffrey as possible and listen to Dad as he explains the latest twist in the maze known as the road to the Olympics.

"The International Federation of Skiing released the news today," Dad begins. "The 2018 U.S. ski jumping team will consist of five male and four female jumpers."

"What a crock!" Jack cups her hands around her mouth and shouts. "I call for a revote! Chicks over dicks! Chicks over dicks! Chicks over d—"

"Enough." Dad interrupts Jack, but not without managing to look like he agrees with her. The truth is not many sports have treated women athletes worse than ski jumping. Hell, we weren't even allowed to compete until 2014 even though we won the right to in 2011. Some bullshit about injuring our internal organs. Like any woman's uterus can't kick any guy in the balls when it comes to surviving stress and pain. Fucktards. Even now, men's and women's ski jumping is far from equal. We can compete in one event compared to the three events for male jumpers, which means less media coverage, which means fewer opportunities to catch the attention of a sponsor. I'm luckier than most. Dad would sell his right kidney before he'd let me miss a major competition, but both Dad and I know it's going to take more than the going rate for spare kidneys to get me to PyeongChang, South Korea. It's going to take endorsement money and lots of it.

"The next International Continental Cup competition is in February at Utah Olympic Park, which is good for three reasons," Dad says. "First, it's one of the best facilities in the United States. Second, ESPN is going to be all over it." Dad looks directly at me. I glare back the silent but clear message that I'm not interested in another one of his *make nice to the reporters* speeches. It's an ongoing argument between Dad and me. He tells me I need to smile pretty for the cameras, and I tell him my jumping speaks perfectly fine for itself, thank you very much. Dad sighs and continues, "And third, it's a helluva lot cheaper to get to Utah than Asia or Europe. Budget for your plane ticket, two nights in a hotel, the competition fee, and the cost of food. Some meals will be provided for you, but not all. We'll fly in on Friday, February 19. There will be two rounds of competition. One on Saturday and one on Sunday, after which we'll fly back home. I'm going to be scoping out the cheapest airfare possible so I need to know who's planning on competing."

I raise my hand, probably unnecessarily. Geoffrey's hand shoots into the air. Figures. He sucks at ski jumping, but he loves the bragging rights that come with competing. Blair, who has never been able to afford travel expenses, sends a questioning glance at Geoffrey who nods, establishing beyond a doubt the true economic value of a blowjob. Blair raises her hand and I look around at the rest of my team, willing someone—anyone—to say they're going. Bogey sends me a sympathetic grin but shrugs his shoulder and drops his head. It pisses me off because Bogey could be great. Really great. But like the rest of the Lab Rats, except of course Sir Moneybags, Bogey's family barely scrapes together enough money to pay Dad's tuition and send Bogey to compete at Hyland in Minneapolis where Bogey kills it every fucking time. I mean, the guy is incredible. But out of state, much less international competitions? Not possible and so not fair. Linnea and Jillian both shake their heads as well, and I turn to my last, best hope.

"That's it," I whisper to Jack. "You're going."

She snorts. "Sure, El. Me and that spare two grand of mine will sign right up."

Dad calls an end to the meeting and wrangles Bogey and Geoffrey into helping him install the new motion-activated cameras along the jump. Evidently Dad has decided that every single move from the inrun to the landing needs to be recorded so he can search for flaws, frame by freaking frame. Wonderful.

It isn't often practice ends while there's still a bit of daylight, so Jillian and Linnea take off. I wish I could, too, but there'll be hell to pay if the exercise room is a mess when Dad gets back, so Jack and I start cleaning up. Blair, whose ride home is halfway up a tree securing a camera, decides she prefers the actual subzero temp outside to our frosty company, which is fine by us.

"Fuck that," I say to Jack as I lift a block and stack it against the wall. "A three-day weekend in Utah alone with Geoffrey-with-a-*G* and Blair? No way. I'm out."

Jack's expression takes on her comic book villain look, arched eyebrow and all. "Don't worry, El. Utah is two months away. That gives us plenty of time to pull off step two of The Blair Bitch Project."

My cheeks flush red at the thought. Jack's idea of revenge sex to take the sting out of Blair's betrayal was fine. Almost as fine as Kate Moreau, but step two of The Blair Bitch Project, a full-on rebound relationship with some girl I dump the minute I'm over Blair? Insanity.

"I don't think so, Jack. I'm good just as I am, thanks."

"Since when does *good* win the gold?" Jack drills me as she picks up a block and stacks it against the wall. "You have to be better than good. You have to be great, El, and you are. You're great because you've got an edge! You know how to shut everything out and give yourself over to the jump, but you can't do that when your head is full of thoughts about what new sexual position Blair and Geoffrey are trying out."

Ouch. Any ref worth their pay would call foul on that comment. I pick up somebody's sweat rag from the floor and throw it at Jack to demonstrate my objection. She catches it on the fly and drops it on the floor.

"El, listen. I'm going to give it to you straight. You've got a real shot the rest of us would kill for." Jack blinks away the tears collecting in her eyes and I'm suddenly not so pissed at her. It's true. The only thing harder than running the marathon to the Olympics is watching from the sidelines. "So don't blow it. Get Blair out of your head and get back to being you. Fucking Eleanor watch-out-world Engebretsen, okay? Pick someone. Anyone. And fuck her brains out until Blair is nothing but a distant memory."

Jack means well. I know she does. But she doesn't get it. I loved Blair. God help me, I still love Blair, which really sucks, and jumping into a new relationship, rebound or not, is one leap I don't know how to take.

"I said no and I meant no." To emphasize how much I want her to drop the subject I pick up another block and toss it across the room where it lands on the floor with a loud thud.

Jack grabs her coat. "Suit yourself, El. The spectator seats in PyeongChang are phenomenal, I hear." It's a cheap shot, out of BFF bounds, but I let it go as she slams the door behind her. Somewhere in that mixed-up head of hers, she's trying to help me.

I slump down on the floor and try to figure out how the hell everything so right went so wrong so fast. The text—that's right. The goddamn text. Has it really only been three days since Blair sent it to me by mistake?

I promise I'll break up with Ellie tonight, Geoffrey. I hate sneaking around as much as you do.

The door opens and Blair comes in, her cheeks blazing red against the white fur that rims the hood of her ski jacket, and when she smiles at me, I almost throw up.

"I thought Jack would never leave." Blair's teeth are chattering. She takes off her coat and walks over to sit on the floor next to me. She's so close I can't help but inhale the scent of her.

"What do you want, Blair?" I stand and grab a block, and yeah, I slam it down next to the others. Dad would definitely not approve of me abusing his equipment, but I don't really give a shit.

I feel her behind me. Her hand on my shoulder burns like I'm allergic to the testosterone she's been soaking up from Geoffrey-with-a-*G*. She turns me to face her and I try to yank away, but she steps in front of me, so there I am, back against the wall, looking into the eyes of the girl I love and the girl I hate. "To talk to you. To make you understand," Blair says.

"What's there to understand? Your text was pretty clear. You got sick of me. Or it was all a lie and you never loved me. Or you wanted something Geoffrey had that I didn't." I spit that last one in her face, because it was always good between us, that part. Better than good.

She reaches up and touches my cheek, my stupid damp cheek. "It wasn't like that, El. I never meant to hurt you."

My body goes in two directions at once. Part of me wants to pull her into my arms. Part of me wants to shove her away. She never meant to hurt me? *She never meant to hurt me?* It balls up inside of me, the anger, and I push away all that is soft and familiar and not mine. Not anymore. She steps back and her eyes fill with hurt.

"El?" Hurt turns to disbelief.

Oh, I'm me, I tell her in my mind. *But not a version of me you've ever known.*

Blair stares at the floor, her long brown-cheating-on-blond hair falling around her face. Her hand disappears beneath her hair like she's wiping away a tear, but I don't care.

Let *her* cry.

Let *her* hurt.

She raises her head and looks at me. Mascara smudges both her eyes. "Who's Kate?"

I almost laugh. Blair wants to talk about Kate? Not the guy she's been banging behind my back for who knows how long? "Why do you care who I fuck?" I shout at her.

"Ellie, please, don't be like this." She holds a hand out to me, but I'm beyond her touch. Beyond her reach. There must be something on my face or in my voice because she takes another step back, her eyes wide.

"Like what? Pissed?" I'm shaking all over. My hands won't stop clenching and unclenching and I get it then, the reason Jack wants me to leap. There's nothing here for me anymore but Blair's lies and Blair's betrayal. The fault line is hers, but I'm the stupid jerk still standing on the ground as it crumbles beneath my feet. Jack, damn it, is right again. I should jump into the unknown, into the meaningless, until I land on my own solid ground where Blair doesn't even exist.

I'm moving around her. Past her. Grabbing my coat and heading for the door. "Leave me alone, Blair. Just leave me the fuck alone."

My thoughts run faster than I do as I head down the driveway and turn left on Highway 61. *She never meant to hurt me?* I'd hate to see what she could have done if she'd put her mind to it. My blood pounds, louder than my feet over the icy road.

My brain is on autopilot as I dart onto the trail that runs parallel with Lake Superior. The path is covered in snow, but I don't mind. Snow has always been my friend. Ice not so much. I run, my breath blasting out in cloudy puffs of air, on instinct and pain. I run because I need to put as much distance between Blair and me as possible.

The trail divides. I can't think. My head is at war between love and hate, but my feet know where to take me. Over the snowy path that leads to the shore of the lake that pretends it's an ocean, the way Geoffrey pretends he's a pro skier. They're both full of shit, but Lake Superior puts on a better show. I reach the rock that juts out over the lake and sit on the cold and hard surface. At least I won't need to ice my glutes tonight. The sunset strikes like a match over the lake and burns itself out until the world around me is nothing but ash. Even so, I do not leave. There's something I need to let surface at the edge of the frozen lake, staring at the roiling waves of ice.

"How?" I gulp in air and it hits my lungs like freezer burn. My vision blurs. My chest tightens. "How could you do this to me?"

I blink and look away from the edge, over the sheets of ice that stretch for miles, until I spot it, the answer in the churning patch of gray blue that never freezes, no matter how cold or brutal it gets.

She could do this to me because I stupidly thought our love was as big and as deep as Lake Superior. I never imagined she could freeze me out. Not completely. Jesus, I was blind.

No more.

"I'm done, Blair!" I scream the words. "Do you hear me? You went too far. I'm done." My cold words splash into the patch of water and freeze shut what had remained open. Like the lake, I feel myself harden all the way through.

CHAPTER SIX

S kating through life is the way Minnesotans get through January, especially once all the lakes are frozen solid, so I strap on a pair and go for it, and it's a pretty smooth ride. Sure, I hit a ripple or two every now and then. I even reached out twice to steady myself in some halfhearted attempt at step two: The Rebound.

One was a blonde. Jennifer? Jordan? Doesn't matter because the whole time I was fucking her, I was imagining Blair. Remembering what she liked and where she liked it and how hard she liked it, so when Jennifer/Jordan came, all I heard was Blair crying out my name. I've never felt shittier or more alone in all my life.

The other was a redhead named Sierra and I thought she had rebound potential right up to the moment when she kissed me. Maybe it would have been okay if I'd kept my eyes open, but how was I to know that closed eyes and soft lips on mine would bring up stabbing thoughts of Blair. I've never ditched a naked girl or a hotel room so fast in all my life.

It's fucking maddening how I see Blair and Geoffrey-with-a-*G* everywhere. Snuggling at Rosie's. Working out at Gravity Lab. Occasionally even in my dreams, but those I don't mind because I get to castrate Geoffrey on a regular basis when I'm sleeping. Eventually I get so pissed I commit fully to step two of

The Blair Bitch Project. If a rebound relationship will make me quit obsessing over Blair once and for all, then I'm in. What I don't see though is the right girl, and believe me, I'm looking. Whenever I'm not throwing myself off the ski jump or listening to Dad pointing out my mistakes—pardon me, my *growth opportunities*—frame by excruciating frame, I'm hitting the slopes at Lutsen. Most days, I'm scoping out tourists, but all I see are silly girls or pouty girls or slutty girls. No one who could interest me enough to take my mind off Blair for one second. Some days I find myself searching for pale blue jackets in a swarm of skiers. I even carry the Eagle Ridge satisfaction survey in my back pocket wherever I go, but I tell myself it's like a drunk's one-month sobriety coin. I'm only hauling it around to remember how long it's been since I binged on self-pity. But one day, after a trek down Freefall, Valley Run, and Mogen, I actually lose my mind and pull out the survey. I stare at the handwriting—no frilly loops or swirls, bold beyond belief. Exactly like her. I even call the number, though I don't have a clue what I'm going to say if she picks up. Probably something stupid like *How's the weather in Tahoe and, by the way, why did I only rate a seven?* but fortunately for me it goes to voice mail.

If you're trying to reach Kate, too bad. Leave a message. Make it interesting and I might call you back.

God, what I wouldn't give to improve Kate's satisfaction score, but that doesn't seem possible so there's no point in leaving a message.

Toward the middle of January, Jack talks me into teaching a SkiWee class with her at Lutsen, and I figure, why not? We both need extra money and there's nothing better than watching a bunch of pint-sized people ski better without poles than their parents do with all their fancy equipment. Makes a person believe that life can be awesome, maybe even fair.

"Could you believe Penguin? The way he killed that jump? Kid's going to be a star someday." Snowflakes land on Jack's windshield and she turns on the wipers.

It's the last class of the day and Jack and I are driving back to Gravity Lab. Neither of us can get over one little guy who was decked out in all black and white and dressed in so many layers the kid waddled. Yes, waddled. I don't particularly approve of Jack nicknaming the kid Penguin, but I can't disagree with her about his talent. Kid definitely could be a star someday. What I don't tell Jack, as she drives north on Highway 61, is that talent isn't enough. Penguin's going to need fanatical family support, an obsession that eclipses everything else in his life, the opportunity to be seen by the right people at the right competitions, and a whole bunch of money.

I don't tell Jack these things because she already knows them too well. Life isn't awesome, much less fair. The gold is out of reach for people like Penguin.

For people like Jack...

She changes the subject. "So?" It's one little word, but I know exactly what she's asking.

"Nobody yet," I reply.

She blows air out through her nostrils and grips the steering wheel. "What are you waiting for?"

Jack has asked me the same question every day for the past few weeks and I still don't have the guts to tell her the only answer that comes to mind. *Someone cocky as hell, preferably with gray-blue eyes and a ring on every finger.*

Jack'd butch slap me for sure and then remind me I don't live in Tahoe.

"That blonde had potential," Jack says.

"Cuddler," I lie, since I've gotten so good at it, and it's an answer that will shut Jack up for sure on the subject.

"Gross." The sign for Gravity Lab comes into view. Jack turns on her blinker and slows the car. "I hate girls like that."

Snow crunches beneath our tires as we turn onto the driveway. The long shadow of the ski jump falls over the car.

Over me.

Less than six weeks. The next International Continental Cup is less than six weeks away.

The thought of a weekend in Utah alone with Blair and Geoffrey confirms how committed I now am to a rebound relationship, though I do need to reevaluate my selection criteria. Maybe narrow it to a girl with a pulse and a sex drive. That ought to make the search easier.

"What about that redhead?"

This time I infuse some truth into the lie. "Too much tongue. Plus, she made slurping sounds."

Jack scrunches her face in disgust as she pulls into a parking space and turns the car off. She swivels in her seat to look at me. "That's it. We're moving to Berkeley, California. I hear the place is swarming with hot babes into other hot babes."

I laugh and open the door. "Sure, Jack. I'll bop inside and tell Dad you and I are trading in our skis for string bikinis. He'll be thrilled."

Jack grunts as she gets out of the car, but I know she's only in a shitty mood because she hasn't gotten any in over two months. Lutsen should host a teen lesbian conference or something for Jack's sake mostly, though I certainly wouldn't complain about it either.

The idea of moving to Berkeley, not to mention taking step two of The Blair Bitch Project, feels like a fantasy as we walk into Gravity Lab. I could use a day off from reality, but Dad doesn't accept a frustrated sex life as an excuse for missing practice.

We're early, and I was expecting Gravity Lab to be a ghost town, but Dad's voice is droning on in the exercise room. One of the Lab Rats must have arrived before us. Poor fool. Jack takes off her coat and shoves her hat and mittens into the sleeves. She turns around to hang it on the hook on the wall while I sit on the bench and start unlacing my Sorel boots.

The sound of Dad's cane tapping on the floor and his booming voice enters the pro shop. "You'd work in the afternoons while

I'm coaching and occasionally on weekends when I'm traveling with the team. Pay's only seven seventy-five an hour, but you get an employee discount on all equipment, and I may even be able to swing a reduced season pass at Lutsen."

Ah, Dad's interviewing someone for the part-time job he advertised. I don't really care who he hires so I don't bother looking up. Besides, the laces on my right boot have twisted themselves into some devil's knot and I'm getting pissed.

"The job's yours if you want it," Dad says.

"I would, Mr. Engebretsen. Very much. Thank you," a girl says, and three things happen simultaneously.

One: My head whips up. Like an innocent little particle floating around in the vast empty space, pre-creation of the universe. Two: Jack slaps me on the back, sending me and my little particle-self sprawling on the floor at the feet of the girl Dad just hired. And three: the girl who happens to be the other little particle floating around in the empty pre-universe space looks down at me, and I consider diving under the bench or bolting for the door, but it's too late.

There's no avoiding the big bang.

"Let me introduce you to my daughter," Dad says and I cringe. "Eleanor, meet our new employee. I'm sorry, what did you say your name was again?"

"Kate." The girl holds a hand out to me and I reach for her before I realize what I'm doing. "Kate Moreau."

She pulls me to a standing position. "Th-thanks," I stammer. Every inch of my body feels like it's being pierced by needles that are either burning hot or freezing cold.

"For picking you up, right? From the floor, you mean. From the floor. You know, where I found you and picked you up," Kate says and I sink into some déjà vu layer of hell.

"Well, I'll be damned," Jack whispers, but I ignore her because Kate is glancing from me to my trophies on the counter to my medals hanging from hooks to the pictures of me competing and back to me and I feel it, the weight of every one of my lies.

"It's nice to finally meet the famous Eleanor Engebretsen," she says. She even smiles, but there's no warmth in it. It's like she's greeting a stranger. "I've heard so much about you."

I should answer. I should explain why I told her I was a tourist, but I can't speak. Can't think. Can't move.

"Welcome to Gravity Lab, Kate." Dad steps between us and takes home the gold medal for Most Oblivious Father Ever. "Eleanor and I are glad to have you join our staff."

CHAPTER SEVEN

Dad, of course, invites Kate to watch practice. I suit up with the rest of the Lab Rats and head out to the jump, but unlike everyone else on my team, I'm carrying something much heavier on my shoulders than long skis—like a half ton of lies and shock.

"You'll need to be able to answer all sorts of questions about our school and the sport of ski jumping," he explains. "No time like the present to see what we do here."

I can think of a few questions Kate's going to have for me, but then I realize I have a few for her, too. Like why the hell is she in Lutsen? And what happened to her living in Tahoe? A surge of heat spreads through my body. Maybe I'm not the only one who should feel guilty about lying.

"When did you move here?" Dad asks Kate when we reach the jump. Thanks, Dad. I can check that one off my list.

"Last week. Mom's financing for her new business in Lutsen finally came through."

Shit. I do remember Kate saying something about a business opportunity her mom was checking out.

Dad nods. "What kind of business?"

"A yoga studio," Kate says. "She's calling it Flex Appeal."

Dad laughs. "Lutsen definitely could use some Flex Appeal."

Oh God, please make it stop. Dad attempting to achieve flirt mode on top of Kate's sudden reappearance? Sorry, but I'm about two seconds away from assaulting an innocent snowbank with a stomach full of vomit.

Thankfully, Dad stops talking about Flex Appeal, which is not to say he stops talking. He step-step-canes it to the front of the jump and goes into Supreme Coach of the Universe mode.

"Ski jumping. It's the easiest thing in the world as long as you can race down a jump at sixty miles per hour and fly the length of a football field. Of course, the sport has changed quite a bit since I competed in the Olympics..."

I hate how Dad's eyes get all misty whenever he talks about his glory days from a million years ago, like anyone cares. He even tucks his cane behind his leg, and I lose it.

"Don't forget to tell her the part where you blew your knee on your landing and lost your shot at a medal—gold, silver, or bronze." I hit low and I hit hard, but I don't care. It's freaking embarrassing.

"El, what are you doing?" Jack whispers, but I ignore her. I'm cold, all the way through my bones. And it's snowing again. And Dad is being a pompous blowhard. And Kate has rematerialized in my life with no warning. And Blair and Geoffrey are making lovey-dovey eyes at each other. And Kate's eyes are roving from Blair to Geoffrey to Jack to me and there's nothing lovey-dovey in her eyes.

Dad wraps up his *I was once an Olympic God* speech and starts practice by climbing the ramp to the coach's stand. Jillian heads to the jump while Kate wanders over to me, casual-like, as if all she wants is to say hello to an old friend. She keeps her voice quiet enough that only I can hear her. Her eyes, she keeps on Blair. "Isn't Barbie over there the same girl we saw in the chalet, the one who reminded you so much of your ex back home?"

I nod. "Her name's Blair, which is kind of close to Barbie now that you mention it."

Kate gives me a look that says she's not in the mood for being corrected. "But she didn't remind you of your ex, did she? In fact, she *is* your ex."

I nod again.

"And Ken Doll?" Her eyes shift to Geoffrey-with-a-*G*.

"That's the guy she dumped me for. His name is—"

"I don't give a shit about him. He's irrelevant." Kate takes a deep breath and exhales. "And the obnoxious one who made me take that stupid survey?" She nods toward Jack.

"My best friend, Jack. She wanted to get your phone number for me."

Kate walks away from the group and toward the edge of the landing zone. Unfortunately, I was born without the gene that understands when a woman wants to be left alone or followed, so I panic. Quietly. Surrounded by my teammates and Dad, I have the most subdued meltdown ever.

In the end I decide to follow her. More accurately, my body decides it wants to follow her.

Kate's all business—shoulders rigid, jaw clenched, staring me dead in the eyes. "You've got one shot at telling me the truth. Why did you lie to me about your ex?"

I know what she's asking. I even know the answer, but Kate's eyes flick toward Blair and miss the look that crosses my face. It's a gift I don't deserve. "Because I was over her. So over her." I almost add the word *honest,* but it would probably get stuck halfway up my throat and choke me to death. Kate says nothing and watches Jillian take the jump and hit a decent flight formation, but botch her landing. It's one of those instances when bad timing can be good timing because I manage to wipe the guilty as fuck look off my face before Kate turns her attention back to me.

"How many times have you and Jack pulled that I-lost-my-keys-on-the-slope stunt?"

The question isn't fair. Jack's answer and my answer are drastically different, but it's a safe assumption she's asking about me. "Once."

Her eyes narrow as she examines my face.

"Once. I swear." My voice is strong and steady. Thank God I put the blonde and the redhead through their horizontal step two auditions in *their* hotel rooms because Kate can never know about them. She'd assume what happened with them was the same thing that happened between us. And sure, fucking is fucking, but nothing could be farther from the truth when it comes to Kate.

Kate nods, which I take as a good sign, but then she hits me with the hardest question of all. "Why did you lie about being a tourist? I mean, what was the point?"

I swallow. There are no technicalities that can get me out of this one. I'm going to have to let her see a truth about me I never show anyone. Not Jack. Not even Blair. "It's hard, you know? Being Eleanor Engebretsen, Olympic hopeful and all that bullshit. I wanted you to like me, Ellie. Just Ellie. Stupid, I know."

Kate's face softens. At least a little bit. "I don't know. Maybe it's not so stupid. Still..."

I rush on before she can linger on that *still*. "Also, you were so hot and I wanted you and it seemed like you wanted me, too, but afterward I couldn't come clean. I wanted to, but it was too late. Fuck, I even called you one day but I got your voice mail and I was too chicken to leave a message."

"Nice try." Kate's eyes narrow. "I'm not that gullible."

I reach into my back pocket and pull out the crumpled satisfaction survey and hand it to her. "See for yourself. There hasn't been a day since you left that I didn't think about you."

She unfolds the survey and looks at it for what seems like forever.

I break the silence. "Are we okay?"

Kate's hand brushes against mine. The effect isn't quite the same through snow gloves, but it doesn't take much to remember her touch.

"We're not...not okay," she says and it settles over us like a dusting of snow. Pretty to watch, even if all it's doing is covering up something ugly underneath, like a bunch of lies.

Dad, in all his horrible timing glory, shouts my name through the megaphone from the coach's stand. "Eleanor, you're on deck."

"I gotta go." I take a few steps away from Kate, then turn back because I hate that I have no idea where we stand. "Would you tell me what the fuck *not not okay* means later?" I ask Kate.

"I won't not tell you," she says and I swear she has the lady balls to smile at me.

I walk toward the jump as Geoffrey hits the takeoff. Too early, as usual. Probably not the only thing he does prematurely. It's a good thought and it distracts me enough that I almost forget Kate is in the audience, about to watch me jump.

I climb the 241 toothy metal steps up the ladder until I reach the platform and step into my skis. I attach the bindings with shaking hands—not from the cold—and sit on the start bar. Even from my perch on top of the jump, I can see Dad standing on the coach's stand and at the bottom of the hill a circle of Lab Rats plus Kate. My pulse races like I've already hit the take off. I skip the part where I let them float away, all the different faces I wear. Blair's betrayed. Kate's one-night stand. Mom's forgotten child. Dad's last shot at gold. I skip the part where I breathe in and out, in and out, five counts in, seven counts out.

I sit my ass down on the start bar and let my skis glide back and forth in the grooves to the rhythm of my thoughts. Blair-Kate-Blair-Kate-Kate-Kate. It happens before I even realize it. She accomplishes with one sassy smirk what the blonde and redhead couldn't do with their hands all over me. Namely, make me forget Blair, if only for a few seconds. I look down at my skis gliding back and forth in the tracks. Kate-Kate-Kate. Could it be that simple? Could the perfect girl for The Blair Bitch Project, step two, show up out of the blue, and if so, am I ready to take this jump?

Only one way to know.

I shove off the start bar and feel the tug of gravity propel me down the inrun, but my shoulders are above my hips and my chest is being pummeled by wind. I push past the wind to align my hips and shoulders, but I lean too far forward and suddenly I'm out of inrun and time for corrections and all that's left for me to do is jump.

I have no sense of how far I fly or how high I soar. I am only aware that I am off balance and flying into a future I can't control. Seconds. That's all I have to get into flight formation and it's not enough. The white ground rises toward me fast, fast, fast and I'm pulling my weight back and spreading my arms and staggering my legs and hoping like hell muscle memory will guide me into a Telemark landing. I land, Telemark-ish, but not anywhere near the K Point.

"Never seen you jump like that before." Jack gives the appearance of praise as I ski up to the team.

Bogey, not bound by the code of best friends, gives it to me straight. "Well, that sucked."

The rest of my team gives me bewildered stares except Geoffrey and Blair who shower me with smug satisfaction. Kate gives me the slightest of smiles, but it's tainted by the disappointment in her eyes.

From the coach's stand, Dad blasts us through his damn megaphone. "Is it too much to ask one of you to show me a proper ski jump today?"

Bogey answers Dad by simply heading to the jump where he nails the takeoff and flies past the K Point. He would have lost some style points in a competition, but not many. Fucking show-off. I'm itching to redeem myself after the first round is over, but Dad limps down the ramp of the coach's stand and calls an early end to jump practice.

"Looks like everyone except Bogey could use more imitation jumps," he says when he walks up to us, and the team groans.

I want to walk back to Gravity Lab with Kate, but Dad nabs her first, leaving Jack and me to trail behind them. We find that sweet spot where we're close enough to hear every word, but not so close it's obvious we're eavesdropping.

"Have you skied Lutsen yet?" Dad asks Kate and she glances back at me before she answers him.

"Once. About a month ago. It was..." She searches for the right word. "Nice."

Nice? *Nice?* She'd better be referring to the skiing because what we did together was better than nice.

Kate continues and I swear I can hear a hint of a smile in her voice. "One run was pretty great while it lasted."

Jack grins and points at me, but that's a leap I'm not going to take. She could be talking about Freefall. Mogen. Valley Run.

Possibly me.

We reach Gravity Lab where Dad and Kate step inside while all the Lab Rats except me secure their skis in the equipment shed. I lean my skis against the outside wall because there's no point locking them up for the night. No way is Dad done with me after that pathetic performance. Hell, I'll probably be jumping by moonlight.

The team heads inside to the exercise room, but Jack holds me back. "Tell me you're going to hit that again."

"As if I'll get a chance." I laugh in Jack's face. "You heard what she said. *Nice.* As in seven out of ten nice."

Jack shakes her head. "I also heard her say you were a great run."

"If she was even talking about me, which she wasn't."

Jack gives me an oh-please look. "You know she was, El. All you have to do is talk her into another run. Simple."

Simple, my ass.

I try to breeze past Jack and her delusions, but she steps in front of me. "You know what to do." Jack places two fingers around her mouth and wriggles her tongue like I need a visual aid.

Which I do not.

A miracle. That's what I need. A miracle that allows me to not lose what's left of my friggin' mind in a world where both Kate and Blair exist.

CHAPTER EIGHT

Somewhere around the twentieth time watching Blair throw herself at Geoffrey-with-a-*G* during imitation jump training, I make a decision. It fucking hurts to think about Blair, and I want to stop giving a shit about what—or more precisely, *who*—she's doing, and Kate might be able to help me with that. I let that thought roll around in my mind for a bit and it picks up speed until I don't simply want to stop hurting because of Blair. I want Blair to hurt. I want her to feel like shit. I want her to see me with Kate and know that she was easy, so fucking easy, to replace. I want her to spend every minute kicking herself for trading down. Jack's right. A rebound relationship is exactly what I need to get over Blair.

But what if it can do more?

I drop into a plank and feel it to my core. How friggin' awesome it would be to get over, get even, *and* get to screw Kate on a regular basis on top of it all. Life couldn't be much better than that scenario. Unless you're Blair. Or Kate, I guess. But Blair deserves whatever she gets, and Kate? I was just a casual hookup for her in December. A seven out of ten. It's not like she ran back into the hotel to ask for my number. She won't hurt long. Not over someone who's a seven out of ten.

No, Kate will be just fine.

Three grueling hours later, Dad finally relents, and by then I'm in true Engebretsen mode—eye on the prize and ready to go for it with everything I've got.

"Kate?" I limp into the pro shop. Sure, my shins are killing me, but the limp is about as genuine as my intentions and I'll take sympathy points if I can get them.

I limp down the aisle of Spyder ski jackets, past the wall of mounted snowboards, around the display of boots, fleshing out the details of how I'm going to approach her. I try to think up the right words to, as Jack called it, take Kate for another run, but I can't stop remembering the night in the condo. What it felt like to be led by Kate and the places she took me, places I never even knew existed. It's a memory that drives me—maybe as much as the need to stop hurting over Blair—through every aisle until it's clear she's not in the pro shop. I head outside, and in the subzero temperature, holler her name.

But Kate's not there.

And neither are my skis.

❖

"Holy shit," Jack says when I tell her my theory about where Kate is and what she's doing. "She's not that crazy, is she?"

I honestly don't know, so Jack and I throw on our jackets, boots, hats, and gloves. I grab the first aid kit, though a few bandages and a tube of Neosporin aren't going to do much good if Kate's insanity ends in disaster.

"Should we tell your dad?" Jack asks, and she's got a point. We should. But he's squirreled away inside his viewing studio, no doubt picking apart my pathetic excuse for a jump. Besides, he and his cane would only slow us down.

Jack and I sprint toward the jump as much as anyone can sprint in two feet of snow. The sun is dipping behind the horizon fast, sending the grounds and everything in sight into deep shadows. Everything, that is, except the jump—the jump, the goddamn motion-lit, motion-recorded ski jump.

Fuck. Fuck. Fuck. Fuck. Fuck. My brain finds and fixates on the pale blue dot climbing the ladder. Up and up and up.

"We should get the megaphone." Jack's suggestion is both exactly right and ridiculously wrong.

I shake my head. "No time. There's no time." Jack doesn't know. Doesn't understand. Kate never stops to take in the view.

A wave of cold hits like I've plunged into freezing water and am treading for my life. My muscles tense. My solar plexus contracts and expands in frantic gulps of breath. I wrap my arms around my body, but not even that can hold me together. An odd response, considering I've known the girl for a grand total of four, maybe five hours.

"Are you sure we shouldn't get the megaphone?" Jack asks and I point my answer.

Two steps to the platform.

One.

She's there.

"Jesus fucking Christ," Jack whispers.

Kate's auburn curls swirl around her face in the wind. She bends over. Puts my skis on the platform. Kneels. No doubt attaching the bindings. Wait, does she even know she needs to attach the bindings? Kate stands and moves in front of the start bar, looks down the inrun. Something rises inside of me. A memory. I'm six years old, maybe seven, standing on the platform for the first time. Looking down at the ground so far away. Looking down the inrun so impossibly steep. It all rushes back as I watch Kate. The nausea. The paralyzing panic. The taste of vomit in my mouth.

What was it Kate told me that day on Mogen?

If you get in trouble, for God's sake, sit your ass down and yell for help.

The voice in my mind needs no megaphone and I swear she hears me because she looks in my direction and juts her chin forward. A challenge? Payback? Whatever, it's fucking stupid. She crouches and throws herself down the inrun, hits the take off point, and flies away. My God, she flies away and I must be dying because no one on earth flies like that. Maybe in heaven, where wings are standard-issue.

It's too late to stop her. It's too late to scream. It's too late to do anything but—

Give her wings, I pray to a God I don't believe in.

And then Kate makes it clear that Dad's been teaching me the wrong lesson all along. It's not about leaning toward death. It's about leaning toward life.

"Holy shit! Look at her go!" Jack says as Kate flies, not away from the jump, but toward the sky.

Eventually, of course, she drops, inch by inch, closer and closer to the hard ground. My mind spins with all the things that could go wrong. I try to close my eyes to pray again, but then I realize I don't have the first fucking clue how to pray even if I could take my eyes off Kate, so I stand next to Jack whose mouth is opening and closing. Hopefully she's saying a silent prayer for all three of us.

Kate touches down. Not even close to a Telemark landing, but a split second later she's steady and strong and slowing to a stop deep in the outrun, arms raised high above her head. She's glowing, not from the lights shining down on her, but from the light shining inside her.

Next to me, Jack starts screaming. "No fucking way! Goddamn, girl, you are something!"

Jack takes off running toward Kate and finally it hits me. She made it. She's alive. And she blew past every single one of my record jumps.

I follow Jack's footsteps in the snow. The door to Gravity Lab opens and a rush of bodies pour out, including my father. Kate's a magnet and she's drawing everyone toward her.

Dad and I reach Kate at the same time and is he pissed. His normal lutefisk-colored complexion has turned snapper red. "What the fuck was *that*?" he swears. My dad who never swears.

Kate bends over, digs her hand into her side, and sucks cold air deep into her lungs. "You said…" She takes another gulp of air. "You said I'd need to answer questions about your ski jump." She straightens when she catches her breath and looks him in the eyes. "Best way to do that was to experience it myself." Kate glances at me and throws a your-turn smile my way. "Seemed pretty easy to me."

The Lab Rats gasp. Dad blinks. Me? I can't help but grin. This fucking girl! Playing the same game, but with higher stakes.

Dad looks at the marks in the snow where she landed, far past the K Point. "I watched your jump on the monitor in the studio, and I have to ask. Have you considered joining the team?"

"Not really," Kate answers. "I came for the job, but jumping with the team could be cool."

Dad scrunches his eyebrows like he has to solve a complex math equation and misplaced his calculator. "I need someone in the pro shop when we're practicing and traveling to competitions. You'd have to pick. Job or the Lab Rats." Dad claps her on the shoulder. "Give it some thought, okay?"

"Don't have to," Kate says. "I need a job more than I need a hobby."

Dad frowns and turns to walk back to Gravity Lab. Knitting is a hobby. Decorating cakes is a hobby. Ski jumping is his religion. Once Dad is out of earshot, the Lab Rats pummel Kate with questions.

"How long have you been jumping?" Jillian asks.

Bogey doesn't let Kate answer. "You are on the team. End of discussion."

Linnea seconds Bogey.

Everyone is drawn to Kate. Everyone except Geoffrey-with-a-*G* and Blair who move away like the limelight on Kate hurts their eyes.

The questions and pressure go on and on and I should probably rescue her, but she doesn't need me. She doesn't need anyone, this girl at the center of it all who laid me bare with nothing but a few rings on her fingers.

Jack grabs my arm and tugs me away toward Geoffrey and Blair. I give Jack a look that says she's nuts, dragging my ass closer to those two, but she grins at me like it's the release date for the *Sports Illustrated* swimsuit edition or something.

"I'm telling ya, El," Jack says, "Kate showing up again is a straight up gift from the sex gods. I'd get busy unwrapping if I were you."

Blair's head snaps toward Jack. "Did you say Kate?"

And I remember why Jack is my best friend.

"Sure did." Jack grins a Machiavellian my-plan-is-working grin.

"As in *Kate* Kate?" Blair's voice pitches higher as she stares at me. Geoffrey-with-a-*G* reaches for her hand, but she slaps it away.

"As in Ellie's Kate," Jack says, and Blair flinches.

It's a completely irrational, not to mention inaccurate, thing to say, but Jesus. Sweet, sweet Jesus.

Ellie's Kate.

I do like the sound of that.

PART III: FLIGHT TIME

Flight time is easy.

In ski jumping.

All I have to do is abandon what was—the jump—and fly toward what I hope might be—a safe landing on the ground. It helps if I hit a perfect flight formation by keeping my arms pointed backward but slightly outward with my hands spread flat, holding my skis in a V to create maximum surface area, and assuming the correct angles. Forty degrees from the horizontal plane to my skis. Sixty degrees above the skis to my legs. And my body? That I keep at one hundred and sixty degrees. Too far forward and I could crash into the slope. Too far backward and I could cut my flight short by getting caught in wind resistance.

Like I said, flight time in ski jumping is easy. All it takes is practice and a working knowledge of physics.

Flight time in real life?

Seems like it should be the same. I mean, lots of people abandon what was for what they hope might be.

Mothers fly to Boston.

Girlfriends fly into someone else's arms.

But that's where the similarities end. In ski jumping, winners succeed by racking up points for both distance and style. Real life doesn't seem to follow that principle.

There are 1544.2 miles between Lutsen, Minnesota and Boston, Massachusetts. That's a helluva lot of distance points. But leaving behind a husband and a daughter who love you? I can't imagine a move like that earning many points for style.

The distance between me and Geoffrey-with-a-*G*? Probably five inches, though I'd bet he lies and says seven. Doesn't matter how many times Blair's flown that particular flight, she still gets laughable distance points. And a text sent to the wrong person? Even fewer for style.

God knows I've gone the distance trying to forgive if not forget both Mom and Blair. Sure, I may have sacrificed a few style points along the way, but nowhere near as many as either of them have. And yet, I still feel like the loser.

Though maybe, with the help of The Blair Bitch Project 2: The Rebound starring Kate Moreau, I won't for long.

CHAPTER NINE

Jack designs a simple, fail-safe plan. Close Proximity + Lots of Exposed Skin + Accidental Touch = Riotous Rebound Sex, which sounds more than good to me, so I waste no time putting the plan to initiate step two of The Blair Bitch Project into action.

Kate's working in the pro shop? I have the pressing need to waltz through on my way to the exercise room in nothing but a sports bra and biker shorts. Time for another jumpsuit? Great. I strip down and try on a dozen in the changing room and the fact that I forget to pull the curtain completely closed is sheer coincidence. The pro shop has a mad rush, which now officially consists of two people or more? I'm Ellie On The Spot, cramming myself behind the register where I bump into and rub against Kate as much as possible.

It should work. It *would* work.

On anyone other than Kate.

Day after day, she's the ideal employee. Perfect attendance. Stellar attitude. Totally professional. Which would be great if I didn't have X-rated hopes for the two of us. Finally, after a week of coming up with excuses to hang out in the pro shop, I lose it and *accidentally* knock over the Dale of Norway sweater display so I can get her alone for longer than three minutes.

Kate isn't even fazed by the mess or the obvious ploy. She tackles the pile of overpriced sweaters while I watch her hands tuck and fold and navigate buttons like an expert.

God, the things I want to do to her.

The things I want her to do to me...

No, I don't ask if she needs help first. I sit beside her and grab a sweater, and we work in silence until I can't stand it anymore.

"You said you'd tell me what the hell we're not *not* okay means." It's more of a question than a reminder, though I don't have the balls to ask her outright.

Kate's hands don't even slow. "It means there are hookups and there are relationships. Different rules apply."

Great. Like that clarifies anything. But I've been doing some research on my own and if I'm right, well, then Kate might have better things to do with her hands than fold wool sweaters.

"I looked it up," I tell her. "Not *not* okay is a double negative, the meaning of which is actually positive. In essence, when you say we are not *not* okay, you're really saying that we *are* okay, am I right?"

Kate laughs, like the fact she inspired me to study grammar pleases her. "I'm saying what we had was okay."

Had. Past tense. As in the night we spent together. My grammar lesson didn't cover how to change past tense to present tense. "I thought it was more than okay."

"Yeah, that part was good." Kate folds another sweater and puts it on the shelf. Me? I can't do anything but stare at her hands and remember.

"Just good?"

Kate stops working and looks at me with a long-suffering expression of someone trying to teach the slowest learner on the planet. "It's only great, Ellie, when it's more than a hookup. We're not *not* okay because I don't know what we are. Do you?"

"I know what I want us to be."

Kate raises an eyebrow. "And that is?"

Easy, uncomplicated—like we were before, but clearly Kate's not interested in casual this time around. "Great," I tell her. "I want us to be great."

"We'll see," Kate says. "I have to figure a few things out first."

"Like whether I'm relationship material or not?" I don't even feel bad putting her on the spot, but like usual, Kate isn't fazed.

"Exactly," she says and reaches for another sweater.

❖

The next day I buy the biggest vase of yellow daisies the store has because 1) I know better than to give Kate some sappy, stereotypical red roses and 2) I spent all my spare money on stupid diamond earrings.

I put them on the Dale of Norway sweater display in the pro shop with a note that says *Made in the USA from 100% relationship material*. It doesn't get more romantic than that, right?

Wrong. Kate is allergic. Not to daisies, but to the idea that flowers can buy affection, though she does take them home with her at the end of her shift and that's got to be a good sign.

"Surprise her," Jack says when I call her that night to whine about how I'm not having riotous rebound sex with Kate. "Tomorrow is Saturday so she won't be working the pro shop. Go to her house and tell her you planned a special outing for her. Don't use the word date. That'd freak her out."

"And then what?"

"Easy. Take her to the most romantic place you can think of. Girls like stuff like that." Jack says this like girls are a foreign species, which sometimes, it feels like they are. "Then make your move."

I lie in bed that night, trying to decide on the most romantic place to bring Kate. I rule out Split Rock Light House. Too many tourists, no matter what time of year. Same with the Gooseberry Falls and Two Harbors. She's seen Lutsen Mountain and Resorts, which leaves only one place. My rock, the one that juts over Lake Superior. But I've never brought anyone there. Not even Blair. I'm not sure why, now that I think about it, but it never occurred to me to take Blair to my spot. The thought hits me, as I feel the tug of sleep, that it doesn't feel odd at all to consider watching the setting sun turn the frozen lake to fire with Kate by my side. Maybe rebound relationships *are* elastic, like they're a rubber band that binds two people together for a short while and it's okay because everyone knows, sooner or later, it's a bond that's going to snap.

A warm front must have moved in overnight because Saturday promises to be the type of January day when anything seems possible, even an early thaw. Around three in the afternoon I head into Lutsen in search of Kate. The sun won't set until five thirty so I have plenty of time to find her and bring her to my rock. Which would be fine…except I realize when I'm halfway to Lutsen that I don't have the first clue where Kate lives. If I'd thought about it, I could have pulled out her employee file in the office and looked it up, but I didn't, so I head to the only other place Kate might be: the future location of her mom's yoga studio. It's pretty hard to miss at the corner of Main and First, with the two-foot banner above the storefront that reads *Flex Appeal Coming Your Way Soon!* I peeked in the window about a week ago, but all I saw was an unfinished space. Kate might be there, helping her mom get the studio ready. I park and stand in front of the store, breathing in the fresh air and courage I need to go in search of Kate. I'm not sure what I'm expecting when I push open the door, but a nose full of sawdust and the stench of varnish definitely isn't it. I'm also not expecting the woman crouched on the hardwood floor in—What's it called? Downward facing dog? Can't be. Her ass'd be sticking up in the air if that were the case. Table pose? Maybe. Except people don't generally wear baggy overalls when they practice yoga. And they don't hold a drippy paintbrush. And they don't scream at strangers.

"Do not take one step closer!" The woman on the floor stops me at the threshold. She has attempted to tie her graying auburn hair back with a bandana, but it looks more like she's propped a blindfold on her head, one that slips down and covers her eyes even as she turns toward me.

"Dammit!" She shoves the bandana back into place, though I wouldn't bet on it staying there. Once she can see again, she looks at me with gray eyes streaked with slivers of blue.

Yep. Kate's mom. Has to be.

"Sorry, we're not open yet." She turns her attention back to the can of wood stain on the floor in front of her. "But there are flyers on the windowsill with details about the open house. Feel free to take one."

I stand there like an idiot, the door propped open by my ass, and try to figure out a way to tell Kate's mom that I'm here to share a sunset with her daughter. Eventually the cool draft reminds her of my presence.

"Can I help you?" She doesn't look up at me as she paints the bare board and the stain soaks in, turning the wood a rich dark walnut. I'm not the most artistic person in the world, but even I can imagine the completed floors and they're going to be amazing. What I can't imagine is why she started at the door. I mean, what's her plan when she reaches the far end of the room? To stand on tiptoe?

"Um, yeah, ah, I was wondering if…"

She must feel me floundering because she stops working and balances her brush on the can. She sits on the unstained part of the floor to look at me. "Are you here to sign up for a yoga class?"

"No, I mean, maybe later, but not right now."

She eyes me up and down, then chuckles. "White-blond hair. Ice-blue eyes," she mumbles, then finds her full voice. "I'm sorry, Ellie, but Kate isn't here at the moment."

"You know me?" Dumb question. Obviously she does.

"Boatload of daisies made in the U.S.? That you?" she asks.

I nod. I'd like to think it's a good sign Kate has described me in such detail her mom can recognize me, but I have my doubts.

She studies me until my cheeks tingle and grow warm. "You don't have the first clue how to handle my daughter, do you?"

She's a friggin' mind reader, but I don't tell her that. I shake my head no.

"Want some advice?" she asks and I almost run over those wet floors to hug her.

"More than anything."

Her eyes take on a serious look. "Don't try so hard."

The half-stained floor seems to tilt. Like the world beneath my feet has shifted somehow. "Wait, what?"

My whole childhood, Mom and Dad pounded one lesson into me. Go for the gold. Never quit. Give it everything you've got. What Engebretsens lack in the way of social graces, we make up in work ethic.

Kate's mom looks at me with the same intense gaze I saw when Kate held me and told me to breathe. "Some things can't be rushed. Take staining a floor for example. You have to strip off the old before you can apply the new. You may even need to sand it right down to its grain. Not the easiest job in the world. Trust me."

What I trust is that Kate's mom is every bit as frustrating to talk to as her daughter. She turns back to the can of stain and dips her brush. It's my cue to leave and I would except for the fact that I still need to find Kate. The sunset isn't going to wait for us.

"Um, I'm sorry." I interrupt her again. "It's just I—I really need to find Kate."

She wipes the brush against the lip of the can, letting the excess drip into it. "She went to Grand Marais to pick up more stain."

I glance at the floor but there aren't any telltale signs of footprints.

"How?" I blurt out.

"How what?" Kate's mom looks up, puzzled.

"How did she walk on the floors without messing them up?"

"She left before I started." Kate's mom looks at the ten feet of dark walnut floorboards that run from the door to where she's sitting. "Well, shit." She yanks off the bandana and pushes aside the flop of curls that fall in her face with dark walnut stained fingertips. "You want some good advice, Ellie? Never take advice from idiotic adults who paint themselves into corners."

I laugh. I can't help it. And I like her. I can't help that either. I reach down and tap a finger on the floor. It's a bit tacky, but not soaking wet. It's possible, this insane thought that popped into my head. Maybe. "Are you going to stain the whole floor?"

Kate's mom looks up at me. "That was the general idea. Why do you ask?"

"Because I have an idea, a crazy idea, if there's even a small patch you can leave unstained."

She looks around, then points at the far left corner of the room. "I'm building a wall of storage cubbies over there. I suppose I wouldn't need to stain underneath them. What's your idea?"

"I was thinking I could put one cinder block where I'm standing and toss another to you. You could put it on the floor where the storage cubbies are going to be. Then I could slide a long board over my cinder block until it reaches yours and we could make—"

"A bridge! A walking bridge! Ellie, you're wonderful!"

No way I'm letting an opportunity like that pass me by. "Don't suppose you could mention that fact to Kate?"

Her laugh comes from her belly. "You got it. After you've stripped off all the old and sanded down to the grain." She stands and the similarities between mother and daughter become even more obvious. Same height. Same athletic build. Same tendency to talk in riddles.

"By the way," Kate's mom says. "I'm Maggie. We should probably be on a first-name basis if we're going to be chucking cinder blocks at each other. Now would you be so kind as to get your ass to the lumberyard before Kate returns? I'll never hear the end of it if she finds me in this predicament."

I do as Maggie asks, and I even beat Kate back to Flex Appeal, which, unfortunately, gives me a first-row seat when she walks in the door.

"What the—?" Kate stares at me, sitting beside Maggie in the small, unstained portion of the floor, admiring the first coat. I expected Kate to be surprised even if we did miss the sunset. I hoped she'd think helping her mom was a sweet thing to do. Maybe even romantic.

Wrong. Wrong. Couldn't be more wrong.

"What are you doing here?" Kate raises her foot like she's going to walk right over those freshly stained floors to tell me exactly what she thinks about finding me in her mom's yoga studio.

I lose the capacity to speak, but Maggie screams loud enough for both of us. "Don't you dare step on that floor, young lady!"

Kate freezes. Takes a beat to think. Withdraws her foot and stands on the threshold where she finds new ways to send wave after wave of rage at me. The only reasonable solution, I decide, is to live the rest of my life in this one little unstained patch of floor, stripping off the old and applying the new every single day, beginning at the door.

Maggie stands and stretches. "Oof, I can Chaturanga Dandasana all day long, but staining floors? That's a workout. Ellie, I can't thank you enough. Kate, isn't it nice that Ellie came looking for you but stayed to help me?"

Kate is eloquent in her silence.

Maggie turns to me. "I hope you like squash."

"What?" My brain cells must still be flooded trying to decode Kate's silent tirade, because I haven't got the first clue what Maggie is talking about.

But Kate does. And Kate does not approve. "No. Absolutely not. Ellie's not coming to our place for dinner. She's way too busy with all those slopes to ski, weights to lift, and tourists to pick up."

That last line pisses me off. It shouldn't, because it's accurate, but it does. In fact, it pisses me off enough to accept the invitation to dinner.

"Squash sounds delicious," I tell Maggie. It's a lie. I hate squash. But it's not the worst lie I've told a Moreau woman.

Maggie and I cross the makeshift bridge to join Kate, who manages to refrain from punching me in the face. Maggie takes one last glance at the gleaming floors, closes up Flex Appeal, and then insists the three of us squeeze into her tiny VW Bug. I offer to drive separately, but she won't hear of it.

"Don't be silly. I want Kate to check on the floors later tonight, so she can drive you back to your car then. It's the least she can do, since you and I did all the hard work." Maggie pops in a Mamas and Papas CD and sings "Go Where You Wanna Go" at the top of her lungs.

"Where do you wanna go, Ellie?" Maggie sings at me.

Down on your daughter doesn't seem like an appropriate response so I say the next thing that pops into my head. "PyeongChang, South Korea."

"Good place," Maggie says. "There's a parrot training school there. Well worth the road trip."

I don't know how to tell Maggie that getting to South Korea isn't exactly a road trip. Also, I'm fairly stumped by the fact that parrot training schools exist and that Maggie knows about them.

"Where do you wanna go?" Maggie sings the phrase to Kate, which Kate ignores, though it's not hard to guess where she wants to go.

As far away from me as possible.

CHAPTER TEN

The VW Bug looks right at home in front of the apartment building where Kate and Maggie live. Someone, about forty years ago, painted the building brown with white trim—I think. It's hard to tell with the paint peeling off the exterior and the rotting window frames.

"It's temporary," Maggie says when we walk up the snow-covered path to the main door of the apartment building. "We're going to buy a house as soon as Flex Appeal takes off, aren't we, Kate?" Maggie tugs the door open.

Kate doesn't answer, which is no surprise. She hasn't said one word since we left Flex Appeal.

Maggie tries to explain away Kate's silence as we step into the apartment building. "She's still upset with me for making her move during the middle of her junior year."

Oh, she's upset, I want to tell Maggie, *but not with you.*

We walk down the dark hallways that smell like fry grease and cigarette smoke. Door after door, we pass the sounds of arguing voices or blaring televisions or screaming babies. It's a glimpse into a life I've never known. Never lived.

We stop in front of a door with a mat in front of it that reads *Nice Underwear* and I laugh. Maggie slides the key into the lock and a deep growl comes from behind the door.

"Don't worry," Maggie says. "That's just Turd."

"Did you say *Turd*?" I ask.

"Ferguson," Maggie says like that explains everything, as she opens the door and a small brown dog launches into my arms. There is French kissing and an exchange of bodily fluids, but not with the make-out partner I had in mind when the day started.

Kate pulls the squirming dog out of my arms while Maggie apologizes. "They kicked her out of obedience school. Twice."

"What a surprise." I wipe the dog drool off my face with my sleeve, at least most of it. "Wait, did you say *her*?"

Maggie nods.

"You named a girl dog Turd?"

Kate puts Turd on the floor where she commences chasing her tail.

"Tell her the story," Maggie says as she walks down the hallway, hopefully to find a bathroom stocked with washcloths.

It's the only chance I may get to talk to Kate alone and I take it. "Okay, I screwed up. Wanna tell me how?"

The look in Kate's eyes says I couldn't be more clueless if I tried. "You decide to hang out with my mom, without asking me if it's okay, and you have to ask how you screwed up?" Kate's voice shakes as she whisper-screams at me, which puts a stop to Turd's tail chasing. "Are you for real?"

"It wasn't like that, Kate. I came looking for you because I wanted to surprise you…" *by showing you a sunset* sounds lame even to me so I shut up.

"Mission accomplished." Kate squeezes as much sarcasm as possible into the two words.

"But, she knows, right? About us. I mean, she knew about the daisies so I thought—"

"No, no, you didn't. Think, that is. You ever have a mom so supportive she tries to hook you up with every cute girl?"

An overly supportive mom? Nope, never had one of those. I shake my head.

"Well, it can be obnoxious. Look, my mom is cool, but I decide who I date. Not her. Not you. And sure as hell not a bunch of stupid daisies. Got it?"

"Got it."

Kate is still bristly and there's more I want to say to her, but then Maggie reappears and hands me a warm washcloth, which cleans up the dog slobber, but doesn't touch the real mess I've made.

"You're not laughing," Maggie observes. "She didn't tell you Turd's story, did she?"

No way am I going to rat Kate out so I don't say a word, but Maggie gives Kate a get-on-with-it look anyway.

"Fine," Kate says. "The dog showed up one night last year."

"It was a Saturday," Maggie adds.

"She was probably a stray," Kate continues. "Tahoe is full of them."

Maggie bends down to pat Turd's head. "She was scrawny and afraid of her shadow and covered in poop. And it was a Saturday night. So we named her Turd Ferguson."

"*You* named her Turd Ferguson," Kate argues. "I wanted to name her Sally." Kate glances at a cat with long gray hair stretched out on top of the couch in the living room. "Ellie, meet Harry."

It takes a second, but then it clicks.

"Great movie," I tell Kate. "Loved Meg Ryan in it."

Kate grins. Or maybe she simply stops scowling at me. Either way I realize I'd profess love for Billy Crystal if it would make things not *not* okay between us again.

"I told Mom no one under forty knows who Turd Ferguson is, but she doesn't believe me."

Turd launches herself on the couch and head-butts Harry who looks like he'd gladly bury Turd in his litter box.

"Not true," Maggie says. "That *SNL* skit was hilarious."

"The one with Burt Reynolds, right?" I blurt out before I realize I've accidentally backed Maggie in this argument.

Maggie slugs Kate in the shoulder. "See? You don't know everything. Sometimes you can even be flat-out wrong about something. Or someone." She tilts her head in my direction. Clearly subtlety isn't Maggie's strength. I can see why it gets on Kate's nerves, but I like Maggie. I even like Harry, the hairy cat, and *Saturday Night Live* and Burt Reynolds and Turd Ferguson, even though she has abandoned the cat and decided to date my left leg.

"Hey." I bend over and look into her blissed-out eyes. "Shouldn't you at least take me out for dinner first?"

Turd barks some reply, drops to the floor, and trots away. Maggie laughs and disappears down the hallway again, leaving Kate and me alone in the living room.

"Not even a burger with fries?" I holler after the dog, though I'm really talking to Kate, which earns me one smile. One tiny-fraction-of-a-second-and-then-it's-gone smile.

"With cocoa?" Kate asks, shocking the hell out of me. If she isn't careful, she's going to remember she likes me.

"Of course. With tons of whipped cream," I answer.

Kate looks into my eyes.

"I am sorry," I tell her. I want to ask for forgiveness, but somehow that feels like too much so I leave it at my apology and wait for Kate to find her way back to me. "Do you want me to leave?"

"In what? Your car's parked in front of Flex Appeal, remember?"

"Yeah, but I can walk to the store. It isn't that far."

Kate scoops up Turd and sits on the couch. "You don't have to do that. Just don't you dare barge into my life without my permission again."

"I won't. I promise," I say. I even mean it.

"Promises are nothing more than hearts waiting to be broken," Kate says. Turd Ferguson sighs in her arms. Behind her head, Harry purrs. Kate has a good life, but something tells me it wasn't always that way.

I'm about to sit beside Kate when Maggie emerges from her bedroom in a pair of yoga pants and an oversized sweater, managing to look fourteen and not forty. She declares me unfit to sit on any piece of furniture and I don't blame her. I may have soaked up half a can of stain with my clothes. I look around the living room for someplace where I can stand without brushing up against anything, which is damn near impossible because Maggie and Kate have filled every square inch of their apartment. They've tossed bohemian pillows and blankets on their odd assortment of furniture. A high-pile rug, the kind that looks like it would make love to your feet, fills their living room. I fight the urge to shed my shoes and socks and take a stroll. But it's the dozen or so postcards on the coffee table that grab my attention. I pick one up with a picture on the front of the largest ball of twine in the world with the words *Lake Nebagamon, Wisconsin,* scrolling beneath it. Everyone in Minnesota knows about the humungous ball of twine and the man who made it, but no one I know has ever bothered to visit it.

On the other side Maggie has written a message to Kate.

Dear Kate,
Whenever I feel tied up inside, I remember how lucky I am to have you as my daughter. Loved unwinding with you on this trip.
Mom

I glance down at the coffee table. At the postcard from Ave Maria Grotto in Cullman, Alabama. The one from Cano's Castle in Colorado. The one from the world's largest jack-in-the-box in Middletown, Connecticut—I can't wait to tell Jack about that place. There are dozens and dozens of them, all to Kate and all from Maggie and not one of them mentions a dad. I steal a glance at Kate, sitting alone on a couch in a one-parent home. Maybe we have more in common than liking girls and ski jumping. Except

Kate has Maggie and I have Dad, and I can't imagine him sending me a postcard or what he'd write.

I flip through them, one at a time, scanning the messages from Maggie to Kate and trying not to look like I'm obviously reading them. I don't want Kate to think I'm barging into her life for the second time in one night, but something about the postcards is irresistible. Is it because they've sought the oddest, weirdest places possible to visit? Or is it because Maggie has sought Kate?

I shuffle through more of the postcards, reading what bits I can until I've soaked up so much love I decide to send Maggie a postcard from the Parrot School in PyeongChang when I'm there. I'm still imagining her face when it comes in the mail, when I pick up another postcard and flip it over.

"Boston's Museum of Bad Art," I read aloud and promptly drop the postcard like it's laced with acid. I take a few steps away and stare at it lying innocently on the coffee table.

Kate decides I need commentary on that postcard of all postcards. "That was one weird place. Seriously, they hung art, really horrible art, outside a men's room in a theater. It was bizarre, but also kinda cool. You should see it if you ever go to Boston."

Thankfully, Maggie pokes her head out of the kitchen and saves me from telling Kate I'd rather choke on a twine ball than visit Boston.

"Dinner's almost ready," Maggie says. "Kate, get Ellie something to wear so the girl can sit down, for Christ's sake."

The scent of butter and brown sugar and cinnamon fills the air as Maggie disappears back into the kitchen. Kate tilts her lap, spilling Turd onto the couch, and stands. I follow her into her bedroom where one wall is wallpapered with posters of the top ski resorts around the world.

Big Sur. Vail. Calgary. Lillehammer. Deer Valley. Whistler. They're all there.

"Lillehammer's my favorite. What's yours?" I ask.

Kate looks away from the wall of posters. "No clue. Never been to any of them. But I can tell you there's a peanut statue in

Plains, Georgia, that honors Jimmy Carter. Bet you didn't know that."

"No, I didn't." It might not be the right time to ask, but she's talking and I don't want to lose her to silence again. "How did you do it?"

"Do what?"

"Blow past the K Point like that. You must have grown up skiing and jumping in Tahoe. Probably even trained with a coach."

"You think so, huh?" Kate opens her closet door and grabs a pair of jeans and a flannel shirt, tosses them on her bed. "Fine. Yes, I've skied and jumped at every resort in Tahoe."

"I knew it! Who was your coach?"

Kate sits on the floor and leans against the wall of posters. Says nothing.

Kate may have invented our stripping game, but I'm not above playing dirty. I grab the hem of my shirt, the one with the built-in bra, yank it over my head, and I stand there in all my nippled-out glory. I even arch my back until I catch Kate looking at me.

"Who trained you?" I ask when I've got her full attention.

"Cassandra White." Kate blinks. Three times fast. She's staring straight at my boobs, but she's not playing our game. In fact, it doesn't seem like she's seeing me at all. It feels like she's far away. Maybe as far as Tahoe. "I guess you could say she was my coach. If it weren't for her I wouldn't know the first thing about skiing."

"Who?" I unzip my jeans and let them fall to my ankles. I step out of them and pull on her jeans. They're a little too big. A little too long. They don't fit—like the name of Kate's trainer. "I thought I knew all the coaches. At least the ones in the U.S., but I've never heard of Cassandra White. Is she new?" I put Kate's shirt on and roll up the sleeves.

She laughs, but there's no joy in the sound. "Cassandra White was a girl I knew in high school. One year her parents bought her a season pass to every ski resort near Tahoe for Christmas. Squaw

Valley, Heavenly, Mt. Rose, Northstar, Sierra, and Kirkwood. She hung those passes on the zipper of her pale blue jacket like they were ribbons she'd won and then she whined because she didn't get the car she wanted instead." Kate's face hardens, and I know she's remembering a girl who grew up taking for granted everything Kate ever wanted. A girl a lot like me. "The coat was too big for me, but the season passes fit just right."

"You stole her coat?"

"Damn straight and I skied the shit out of those season passes." She doesn't look at me. Won't look at me. "I ski jumped, too. About half a dozen times before the season ended."

My brain explodes. Half a dozen times? Did she say *half a dozen times?* Impossible.

I hate that Kate had to steal her way onto the slopes. I hate that I never had to. I hate that Kate still has to ski in Cassandra White's pale blue jacket. I sit down beside her and reach for her, but she pulls away.

"I don't think so, Ellie. Not this time." She stands and walks out of her bedroom, leaving me fully dressed but stripped raw.

❖

Maggie's squash isn't bad. It isn't great, but I take seconds anyway, and it seems to make Maggie happy. She's full of chatter about how she's going to put in a sound system and paint wall murals and throw the most epic open house Lutsen has ever seen. While I don't mind listening to her plans for Flex Appeal, I do mind when she brings up the one subject I was hoping she'd forgotten.

"So, Kate." Maggie puts down her knife and fork. "Ellie tells me you were invited to join the Lab Rodents, but turned it down. Why?"

I'm not sure if I should laugh at Maggie renaming the team or cry because Kate looks pissed again.

"It doesn't matter." Kate pushes her plate away. "Drop it."

Kate's tough, but it's a trait she inherited from Maggie.

"Bullshit. Why don't you want to join the ski team?"

Kate stares at the kitchen table and says nothing.

Maggie turns to me. "Fine, she won't talk. You will. Spill. What's going on with the Lab Rodents, and why doesn't my daughter want to join them?"

"Lab *Rats*," I answer, knowing that each word I say is shredding my promise not to barge into Kate's life without her permission. "And I don't know why she won't join the team. She's an amazing jumper."

Kate cuts me off. "Stay out of it, Ellie. This is none of your business."

But it is my business. Promise or no promise, Kate has to be a Lab Rat. She has to go to Utah, and she has to go as my girlfriend. I need her to go, goddamn it. I need her beside me.

I ignore Kate and turn to Maggie. "One jump. She qualified for the team in one jump. First time that's ever happened. She's that good."

Maggie puts a hand on Kate's arm. "I don't understand. You love skiing. Why would you turn down an opportunity like this?

Precisely. Going to Utah is an opportunity for Kate and a damn good one. Unless she wants to spend the rest of her life looking at posters of ski resorts instead of visiting them in person.

Kate shakes off Maggie's hand and pushes back from the table. "Do you know how much tuition at Gravity Lab costs? Ask her."

Maggie looks at me, the question in her eyes and when I say the number she flinches.

"Besides, I can't work at the pro shop and be on the team. Coach Engebretsen was clear about that. Something about a scheduling conflict."

What the hell, I'm already on Kate's shit list. "Actually, I have an idea that might change that." It's a leap, but I've taken worse.

Kate looks at me like she's about two seconds away from breaking my nose. Maggie looks like she might hug me. It's a confusing moment, to say the least.

"Don't you dare." Kate shakes her head.

"Do it," Maggie says. "If you can make this happen for my daughter, do it."

❖

Later, much later, I lie in bed, trying to figure out how to approach Dad in the morning. Kate and I may have missed the sunset, but the day wasn't a total loss. I won over one of the two Moreau women. Two if you count Turd.

But I'm not quitting. No way.

Not until I've won over all three.

CHAPTER ELEVEN

How can she work the pro shop and practice with the team, much less travel to competitions?" Dad sounds completely uninterested. He hits rewind to watch my ski tip judder out of position. Again. He's got me trapped in his viewing studio, a small room that used to be a large utility closet, for another frame-by-frame session of *Let's Find Eleanor's Mistakes—I Mean, Opportunities for Improvement.* The air reeks of Dad's feet, my sweat, and the lingering scent of Pine-Sol. I'm sick to death of having every one of my flaws magnified and dissected, but at least I'm used to that. I'm even sicker of him being an obstinate ass and not seeing the brilliance of my solution.

"Reality check, Dad. Kate can't afford the tuition any other way. You can have her as an employee, but not as a member of the team if you don't let her work the tuition off." Dad's face pinches at the thought of training someone for the stingy price he pays his employees. He needs to remember what I will never forget. "You did watch her jump, didn't you?"

Dad hits the stop button on the footage of my last jump and cues the video of Kate. Watching Dad watch Kate brings up an emotion I can't describe. Something between the desire to sing "Look at Her Go" and the feeling that I'm going to vomit. She's good. Fuck, she's great.

Dad hits the stop button, freezing Kate as she launches into the air.

"Her ankles aren't cocked." He states this fact like it's a class one felony. He hits play again and examines every second of Kate's jump. "She's throwing away style points left and right. And what kind of landing was that?"

"What you're looking at is the seventh jump in her life," I tell him.

Dad startles. "Seventh?" His face floods with disbelief. "Must be some sort of a fluke."

"It isn't. I've seen her ski, Dad. She's a natural. A once-in-a-lifetime born-to-ski natural, and you could be the one who discovers her."

He grunts. Leans back and crosses his arms, assuming his convince-me stance.

"All you have to do is rearrange the schedule so she can work in the pro shop and be on the team." I don't say more because I don't have to. He's already introducing himself as Kate's coach in his mind.

He hits the stop button and the screen blinks black. Good-bye Kate. He swivels in his chair to face me. "She's completely raw. She's going to need more training than a few after-school hours."

I've anticipated this problem. Even hoped for it. "Agreed. Which is why I'll train her after practice. Before school. Whatever it takes. I don't mind."

Talk about the understatement of the year.

"And what about your training schedule? I don't need to tell you how important the International Continental Cup is for us." *Us*, he says, like he's going to take the jump with me and impress some sponsor. Not likely. Still, he's frowning as if he's picturing a river of gold slipping between his fingers.

"I'll train with her. We'll review all the basics together. Might even be good for me."

He looks skeptical.

"Aren't you always preaching the importance of remembering the basics?"

He frowns, like it pisses him off having his words used against him, but then he speaks, and I figure out he's frowning because he's thought of a detail I haven't. "Does she even own a pair of skis?" he asks.

Fuck. He's right. Kate had to rent her downhill skis. No way does she own ski jumping equipment.

"How tall is she?" Dad asks, though I'm not sure why.

"About five seven." It's a guess, but I've seen every inch of her, so it's a pretty good guess.

He stares into space and I'd pay almost anything to know what he's thinking. Then he inhales sharply and blows his breath out hard. "Close enough. I suppose Kate could use your mother's skis. At least until she comes home."

I don't think I've ever felt more love or more pity for Dad than at that moment.

"But what about Utah?" he asks, breaking my warm and fuzzy feeling for him. "What's the point of training her for free if she can't afford to compete?"

Crap. I was hoping he wouldn't think of that complication. It doesn't feel right, lying to Dad after he basically gave Kate Mom's skis, but what's that saying? I have to be cruel to be kind? Maybe I have to lie to tell the truth.

"She said she can go. Sign her up." The lie is, Kate never said any such thing. The honest part is, she will. *If* I can find the receipt and *if* the store clerk is in a post-Christmas *go ahead and return them I don't really give a fuck* mood and *if* I can figure out a way to pay for Kate's airfare, competition fee, and two nights in a hotel without her finding out, and *if* Kate will ever forgive me for barging into her life again.

That's a lot of ifs.

Yet there's no doubt the diamond earrings on my nightstand cost enough to send Kate to Utah. There's no doubt she deserves to go. There's also no doubt I would love to spend the weekend with Kate, especially if it makes being around Blair tolerable.

Which it will.

All the better if it makes Blair miserable.

Dad grabs his cane and grunts himself into a standing position. The search for *Eleanor's Mistakes—I Mean, Opportunities for Improvement* has apparently ended along with the discussion.

"Be sure she strengthens her ankles. They look weak," he says. It's the closest to *fine, you win* he's going to give me and I take it. Gladly.

"Dad?" I stop him at the door. "Thanks."

He dips his chin and limps toward the pro shop, presumably to perform some scheduling magic that will allow Kate to both work the pro shop and practice with the team. I don't care how he does it. I only care that Kate and I will be spending hours and hours together. Hours that I won't be thinking about Blair. And if I'm lucky, hours Blair will spend thinking about me, for once.

❖

I don't know if I should be excited to tell Kate the news or if I should be dreading it. It could go either way. Why am I so nervous? I barely brake as I round the curves on the road into Lutsen. Pretty damn stupid considering the conditions of Minnesota roads in January, but I arrive at Flex Appeal in one piece. How long I'll stay that way remains to be seen.

I open the door and am immediately smacked in the face by paint fumes, though they are less abusive than the varnish and sawdust I inhaled the last time I was here.

My timing couldn't be better. Maggie and Kate are painting the last wall in the studio. They've already trimmed the ceiling and floorboards, so all that's left is the rolling.

"Wow, it's beautiful!" I say and I'm not only talking about the paint job. I'm talking about the crystal and porcelain doorknobs attached to the wall by the front door at perfect coat-hanging height. The new reception desktop built with a repurposed antique door.

The paper lanterns hanging from the ceiling for muted lighting. All the details Maggie and Kate have loved into the place.

"We're building the cubbies tomorrow," Maggie says, as she rolls another streak of paint on the wall. "They'll cover that patch of wood that looks as unstained as a pair of new underwear."

I'd ask Maggie if she'd like help with the cubbies, but I know her answer. *Of course.*

I also know Kate's. *Not from you.*

The walls make me think of lying on my back on a summer day, grass tickling my legs and arms, while clouds float overhead. "Awesome color."

Maggie beams. "Ask me what it's called. G'head. Ask!" Fortunately Maggie is too impatient for me to guess names of paint colors, because I've got nothing better than blue gray.

"Meditation!" She grins. "How could I not buy a paint called meditation?"

"You couldn't," I tell her. "It would have been unthinkable."

"Exactly." Maggie turns toward Kate who is thoroughly ignoring my presence in the yoga studio. "Did you hear that? Ellie agrees with me." Maggie turns back to me and whispers, "Kate wanted a shade called *I've got the blues*, but I couldn't choose that. Who would come to a depressed yoga studio?"

I'm already doomed. Might as well get on one person's good side. "Nobody. Not a single soul."

Kate slams her roller into the tray, sending paint spraying onto the plastic floor covering.

Maggie returns to the wall and picks up a paint roller. Kate has made her feelings clear, but that doesn't mean I'm leaving. There are things to say. Important things. Good news type of things, and damn it, Maggie and Kate are going to hear them—as soon as they've finished the wall. Sure, I feel like a total schmuck, sitting on the floor and watching them work, but I'm not going anywhere near Kate as long as she's armed with a saturated paint roller.

Maggie rolls a stripe of paint from the pre-trimmed ceiling all the way to the pre-trimmed floorboard, then kneels to dip her roller in the pan. Kate steps around her mom and paints another stripe with enough overlap to blend into Maggie's stripe. Kate kneels to reload her roller while Maggie steps around her and paints another stripe from ceiling to floor, and so they paint. Swapping places, in perfect sync, and blending into each other. They're the painting version of a goddamn Olympic couple's figure skating team. All they're missing is the glittering costumes.

It wells up in me then, the hurt that skates the edge of my anger. *Mom*. Who leaves her family like that? Who up and packs and moves across the country without even saying good-bye? Who doesn't even bother to call, much less send a fucking postcard?

My throat burns. Damn paint fumes. I'd leave, but they're painting the last stripe, so I tough it out. Maggie and Kate set down their rollers in unison and step back to admire their work.

"Not bad, kid," Maggie says, but Kate has seen enough of the wall and turns to me.

"Why are you still here?"

"Ellie can come here anytime she wants," Maggie says. "I pay the rent on this place. Don't you forget it."

I cringe. Maggie means well, but shoving me in Kate's face is not going to score me any points with her. I hate the thought, but taking a break from Flex Appeal for a while might be a good idea.

Kate ignores her mom and walks over to me. "No, really. What do you want?" There's nothing remotely meditative in her blue-gray eyes.

I tell her anyway. "Dad said he'd waive your tuition if you'll agree to work in the pro shop for free."

Kate takes a step backward. "Why would he do that?"

Maggie crosses the room and pulls me into a hug. "You talked him into it, didn't you?" She whispers in my ear. I nod, not trusting my voice. I don't remember the last time I felt a mother's arms around me.

"You wonderful, wonderful girl. Kate is so lucky to have a friend like you." She squeezes hard, too hard, and I break away. She can't talk about me like that. She wouldn't. Not if she knew the real reason I want Kate to go to Utah is because I need a shield between me and Blair. Or is that the real reason? I'm suddenly not sure about a lot of things.

Maggie turns to Kate who still looks stunned. "Did you hear that, Kate? You're a Lab Rodent!"

It should be a funny moment, but it isn't. Not with my throat burning again from the stupid paint fumes and Kate looking like she'd rather choke me than thank me for making her dreams come true.

Hurt floats to the surface of her eyes, then sinks back into the pool of rage. "You promised to stop barging into my life. I never asked for special treatment. Who do you think I am? Some fucking charity case?" She holds her hands at her sides in fists so tight I can almost feel her fingernails digging into her skin.

"You're not a charity case. You're a damn good jumper and you deserve to go." I've seen her wall of posters. I know where to fling my words. "You belong there...with me." Who knew I could aim for her weak spot and hit mine instead? Especially when I didn't even know I'd developed one for Kate.

Her body stays rigid, but her hands slowly unclench. "I suppose you expect me to thank you."

"Not at all." I hold her gaze so long it turns into a who-can-blink-last contest, and for once, after all the stupid games we've played, I win. "You're perfectly free to go in tomorrow and tell my dad to fuck off and keep the paychecks coming. Fine by me. But the opportunity is yours, in case you're sick of wondering whether or not you could be great. If you want to find out, be at my house at six a.m. tomorrow morning."

"Fuck you, Ellie," Kate says, but her eyes aren't pissed. Not even close.

"That opportunity is yours for the taking as well. Anytime. Anywhere." I blurt the words out before I realize Maggie is still standing right there.

Kate gasps and I get ready to duck, but then Maggie chuckles and answers the very question I'm trying not to ask myself. "You two are perfect for each other, that's for damn sure."

"Mom!" Kate looks horrified. "How many times have I asked you to—"

"Yeah, yeah, I know. Butt out of your life." Maggie grins. "Especially your *love* life. Well, guess what? I'm your mother, and it's in the contract all mothers sign, otherwise known as a birth certificate. We breathe and push and it hurts like hell, but in the end we get a baby and in exchange we promise to love you and watch over you, and even drive you crazy if that's what it takes to make sure you're safe and happy. Sorry, there's no fine print in the contract."

The light from the window falls across Maggie's face and she's a mess, a wonderfully splattered gray-blue meditative mess.

She's also wrong.

There's plenty of fine print in the contract.

CHAPTER TWELVE

The sun in Sunday hasn't shown up yet, but Kate does. Dark and early and right on time. Tchaikovsky's concerto, the second movement, blasting from the living room, drowns out the sound of her VW's tires crunching over the snow in the parking lot so she catches Dad and me off guard.

"Hello? Anybody here? Coach Engebretsen? Ellie?" Kate's voice travels up the stairs from the pro shop below. Dad, sitting at the counter in his underwear and bathrobe, frowns at me. When did the wrinkles in his forehead deepen into craters? It can't have been overnight. Can it?

"What do you want me to do?" I ask him.

He twists the wedding ring on his left hand. "Handle it."

I nod and he picks up the fat envelope, the one with the Boston postmark that arrived in yesterday's mail, and shuffles down the hallway to his bedroom.

Mom finally made it official and sent Dad divorce papers. Why now? Because she's plucking the strings of a cellist named Bernard. Talk about a breach of contract.

"Up here," I call to Kate. On any other day I'd love the sound of her footsteps climbing the staircase to my apartment.

Today? Today, I'd really like Kate to go away.

"You said six a.m., right?" Her voice comes from the living room. It's full of life and energy and hope, all the things that have abandoned the Engebretsen household.

"Be right there." A quick glance downward before I leave the kitchen tells me I'm quasi-presentable in my white tank top and maroon flannel sleep pants. It's cold in the apartment and my tank top is tight, another thing I wouldn't mind on any other day, but tempting Kate is the last thing on my mind.

I find her in the living room standing in front of the window where the sun is rising over Lake Superior, backlighting the evergreens and Kate's face. She's staring at the pair of skis and boots I wrapped with a bow last night and leaned against the wall next to the window.

For Kate, from Eleanor and Coach Engebretsen. Welcome to the team. Dad wrote the words on the tag himself. Even he knows the skis are a gift, not a loan.

"It's—it's too much." She turns to examine the skis. They're top of the line and never been used. A gift from my father last Christmas. Mom wanted a new violin instead. I can still hear the fight that followed in my mind.

"It's no big deal," I tell her. "Someone left them behind."

Kate turns around and her face is incredulous. "How could anyone do that? Forget something so valuable? I don't get it."

I don't either so I sink onto our couch and Kate sits beside me except it isn't our couch. It's Dad's shitty futon, bought to replace our couch Mom took with her to Boston.

"I guess it's easy to leave behind things you don't care much about." My voice gets softer the longer I think about my mother. "Or never wanted."

"What?" Kate asks. Tchaikovsky is still blasting out of the sound system. Kate taps the off button and the last bit of my mother fades away. "What did you say?"

"Doesn't matter," I tell her and we sit in the shadow of Mom's skis, on Dad's shitty futon, and watch the glowing globe of fire rise off the lake and climb into the sky. Kate even puts her arm around my shoulders and it feels good. Too good.

"You ready to earn those skis?" I ask her.

"Yeah, of course," she nods. "Let's go hit the jump."

She's itching to fly and I don't blame her, but jumping isn't what I have in mind for Kate's first lesson.

"Later. Today you learn the basics. Follow me." I stand and lead her downstairs to the exercise room where I fling open the equipment closet.

I haul out the hurdles and place them three feet apart along the entire distance of the exercise room, five in a row. Then I return to the cupboard and pull out the board with wheels. It's one square foot, and it's a motherfucker to master.

"You want to be on the team? Fantastic. Here's your first lesson. Ride this board until you reach the first hurdle. Jump the hurdle while the board glides underneath it and land on the moving board. Keep going until you clear all five without taking out any of the hurdles or missing the board. Understand?"

I hand the wannabe skateboard to Kate. She looks at it, then at me.

"This is a joke, right?" she asks.

"No joke."

Kate eyes the five hurdles again, all set to four feet in height. "Impossible. No one can do that."

"Wanna bet?"

"Depends. What are we talking about?"

I grab the board out of her hands and toss it on the floor. "I clear all five the first time without missing the board and you owe me three dates."

Kate looks at the tiny board, at the hurdles, then at me. "One date."

"Deal." I step on the board and crouch down. One kick of my left foot sends me racing toward the first hurdle where I spring up, up, up, and over, while the board glides beneath the hurdle. I land solidly on the board and cruise toward the second hurdle.

Behind me Kate gasps. "Holy shit!" But I keep my eyes straight ahead. She hasn't seen anything yet. I clear the second, the third, the fourth, the final hurdle, and I don't even break a sweat.

I lean my weight on the left side of the board, taking a nice wide arc back to Kate.

"Now you." I jump off and let the board glide up to her. She stops it with the toe of her shoe and looks at me with something I haven't seen before.

It might even be respect.

"What the fuck did I get myself into?" Kate mumbles as she kicks off toward the first hurdle. She clears it and lands on the board, but then she tries to clear the second hurdle and her left foot clips the bar, sending it and Kate crashing to the ground.

"What does any of this have to do with ski jumping?" Kate asks as she rubs her ass and stares at me.

She may as well learn early on not to question her coach, so I chase down the board and bring it back to her. She reaches for me and I yank her into a standing position. "Again," I tell her.

This time Kate clears the first, second, and third hurdles, but misses the board on the fourth and lands on the ground. "Fuck!" She winces and hops on one foot. For once I agree with Dad. Her ankles do look weak.

I retrieve the board and put it in front of her. "Again," I tell her. "And this time pay attention to your feet. Visualize landing on the board."

"Sure, sure," Kate grumbles. "Pay attention to the hurdles. Pay attention to the board. Now I'm supposed to pay attention to my feet, too?"

"Precisely," I answer.

Kate shoots me a dirty look, then crouches on the board and stares at the hurdles. For the first time ever, I see a moment of hesitation. One split second of doubt.

"I bet Cassandra White could do it," I yell at her and it works. She clears four hurdles before she takes out the fifth.

As the hours go on, I learn a few things about Kate. First, her vocabulary of profane words is impressive. Second, her ass is going to need serious icing tonight. And third, she does not give up.

Not on her sixth try. Not on her sixteenth. And on her seventeenth attempt she clears all five hurdles.

"Fuck yeah!" Kate kicks the board in a manner Dad would definitely not allow, sending it flying into the air where she catches it, and walks over to me.

"Well?" she asks.

"Not bad," I say.

"Not bad? That's it? Not bad?"

"Quit bitching," I tell her. "And do it again."

By noon, I send Kate home with the promise (threat?) that I'll pick her up for our date at six thirty, though to pull it off, I'm going to need help. Specifically, Jack's help.

I dig out my cellphone and call Jack before Kate's even backed out of the parking lot. "Major SOS situation over here. Is there anything remotely interesting to do in Lutsen tonight?"

Jack's laugh comes through the phone loud and clear. "In Lutsen? You serious?"

"So serious. I've got a date with Kate, and I'm desperate."

"Impressive," Jack says, "I thought it would take you a few more weeks to sweet talk her. She must have lied on her satisfaction survey."

Jack will never, as long as I live, learn how I tricked Kate into a date.

"Yeah, yeah. I'm impressive as hell. Do you have any ideas or not?"

The silence on the other end of the phone feels like it goes on for hours. "I suppose we could drive to Duluth and go to a club."

"We?" Jack tagging along on my date with Kate is definitely not what I had planned.

"Yes, *we*, because *I* am the one whose cousin checks ID's at Pandora's Box and *I* am the one who banged the bartender—actually both bartenders—which means we won't be drinking Sprite all night."

"Pandora's Box?" I try to picture Kate, Jack, and me clubbing it at a lesbian bar. Not exactly what I had in mind, but it's better than the nothing that is happening in Lutsen.

"Okay, I'll pick you up around seven," I tell Jack, as I climb the stairs to the apartment. Dad's door is still shut so I head into the kitchen and make grilled-cheese sandwiches and tomato soup, which pretty much exhausts my culinary repertoire.

I knock on his closed door. "Dad?" No sound comes from inside his bedroom. "I made lunch."

I hear a grunt and then a squeak from the mattress and then the floorboards echo as he crosses his bedroom. He opens the door. "I'm not hungry," he says.

"Tough shit," I tell him. "Get your ass in the kitchen and eat a damn sandwich, and when you're done with that, how about you make friends with your shower?"

Dad nods and heads toward the kitchen.

Sometimes it takes an Engebretsen to know how to deal with an Engebretsen.

Dad eats his sandwich and drinks the soup. He even digs up enough attitude to give me shit about the thirty grams of saturated fat we're both eating, which is fine by me. If he's bitching about nutrition, he's focusing on staying healthy—at least, part of him is.

"I was thinking I'd go to Duluth tonight with Jack and Kate." The question is implied, but not because I need his permission. As long as I'm hitting the K Point and not flying like a floundering albatross, Dad pretty much leaves me alone, but tonight is different. I'm not sure he should be alone.

His answer is a grunt, which I interpret as yes, since Dad has no difficulty pronouncing the word no.

"'Kay, thanks, Dad." I gather up the plates and bowls, open the dishwasher, and get ready to make space where none exists, but Dad stops me.

"Since when do we skip rinsing our dishes, Eleanor?"

Yeah, he's going to be fine.

I rinse the dishes while Dad rinses himself in the shower, and when we're both done, we meet in the living room. He turns on that CD again and I don't have the heart to turn it off, but I also can't stand listening to one more rendition of Irina Engebretsen the Wonderful. I grab my coat, too light for a walk but perfect for a run, and head toward the stairway that leads down to Gravity Lab.

"Going somewhere?" Dad mumbles, but he's not looking at me. He's staring at the fat envelope in his hands again.

"A run," I tell him. "Need to burn off those thirty saturated fat calories."

Dad grunts his approval.

I don't tell him I also need to burn off the anger I can't express at a mother who isn't there. Dad may be able to lose himself in the shuffle of legal-sized paper, but I have only memories, and I don't dare lose myself in those. So I take it to the road, my anger and my hurt. It's a brisk nose-hair-freezing day. Perfect for chilling out, one pounding step on the pavement at a time. Five miles in, I'm not sure, maybe ten, I feel the tension in my muscles finally release. I glance at my watch. My heart rate of 126 is perfect, but the time of four p.m. is not. I'm going to have to haul ass if I'm going to make it home in time to get ready. It's been a day full of hurdles and I still have to clear the toughest one of all: figuring out what the hell to wear on a date with Kate.

CHAPTER THIRTEEN

Picking an outfit has driven me to stress-eat junk food, specifically chocolate, my go-to therapy of choice, a bad habit I picked up from Blair. I'll never forget the first time I watched Blair eat a candy bar. It was in Rosie's Chalet and we'd been skiing for hours, and every part of her body was screaming for a hit of sugar. Blair grabbed the first candy bar she saw—it might have been a Mounds. I'm not sure, because she ripped that wrapper off before I could even see it, popped the candy in her mouth, and spent the next ten minutes moaning.

Yeah, I never worried about what to wear for a date with Blair. Clothes. Candy wrappers. She treated both the same.

But this is Kate, and I have no clue about her opinion on candy bars. What if she picks them *based* on their wrappers? What if she tears them open slowly and inches the candy out, bit by bit, nibbling as she goes?

It's a damned stressful thought as I stand in my bra and underwear in front of my closet, scarfing my third Snickers bar and staring at every item of clothing I own and now despise. Also, my reflection in my dresser mirror is scaring the shit out of me. What the hell happened to my hair? Have I stood in front of my closet so long that my hair actually dried in those crazy white-blond spikes? One tap with the palm of my hand tells me I absolutely have. My alarm clock tells me there's no time for another shower. My closet tells me I still have no idea what to wear, but I'm out of time so I have to put on something. Anything. Kate is expecting me to pick her up in less than twenty minutes, wearing actual clothes, and to make it worse, she doesn't know about Jack.

God help me, she doesn't know about Jack.

I am so fucked.

Desperate, I dig out the pair of ripped jeans, the ones Blair resurrected by calling them peekaboo sexy.

It seems impossible, but it's almost a year ago Blair talked me into buying the damn jeans. It was the day of the wicked snowstorm, eight inches in under two hours with thirty mile per hour winds coming straight off the lake, but Blair was in mall withdrawal and begged me to go with her to Duluth.

To shop.

It was the type of torment I was willing to endure back then, but only for Blair Caldwell. One year of walking around with a hard-on will do that to an otherwise sane woman. It'll make her drive through impassable conditions. It'll make her pretend she loves being dragged into store after store. It'll make her strip on command in order to try on obscenely overpriced jeans in cramped dressing rooms in front of the girl of her dreams—the supremely uninterested and presumably straight girl of her dreams.

"Oh. My. God. Look at your ass!" Blair squealed.

Yes. *Squealed.*

I did the obligatory 180-degree turn and cranked my head to stare at my ass in the mirror.

Except my ass, glorious as it might be, wasn't what caught my attention. It was the look on Blair's face, the look I'd given up hope of ever seeing.

"I don't know. Should I get them?" I fully admit to arching my back to highlight my assets at that moment. Girl's gotta do what a girl's gotta do, right?

"Uh-huh. Def. You have to," Blair said, her gaze not leaving my ass for one second.

So I bought the damn jeans. I didn't need another pair, especially ones that came with a hundred-and-sixty-dollar price tag, but I did need to see that look again on her face, that priceless look.

Blair, usually so capable of filling the smallest second with chatter, sat silently beside me the whole way back to Gravity Lab. I didn't talk either, and not because I was gripping the steering wheel and praying like hell I wasn't aiming the car at the ditch. I didn't talk because I didn't have words to express what I was feeling. Unless I wanted to talk about global poles reversing. Tectonic plates shifting. Suns, somewhere far away in the vast universe, imploding. The electrifying feeling that everything could change. Was changing.

Somehow I navigated the whiteout conditions and we made it back to Gravity Lab. Blair led the charge up the stairs to our apartment with me trailing behind her. I wasn't in as much of a hurry to explain why I'd spent nearly two hundred dollars on jeans I didn't need. "Mrs. E, you gotta see the jeans El bought!" She burst into the living room. "Mr. E, what's going on?"

Those were the last words I heard before I caught up with Blair, bag-o-jeans swinging in my right hand. Before I found my father sitting on the floor where the couch should have been. Crying. My father who never cries. Before my world imploded.

"Mr. E?" Blair asked again. She took a step toward Dad while the avalanche of evidence hit me. Half-empty bookshelves. A rectangular patch, one shade darker than the rest of the wall. What had hung there? A family portrait, the one taken of us in Switzerland? Yes, that was it.

Since when do robbers steal family portraits?

"Are you okay, Mr. E?" Blair touched his shoulder and Dad pulled away.

My mind flooded with details. No steaming cup of tea on the coffee table. No coffee table. No fleece slippers tucked under her reading chair by the window. No reading chair.

"Dad, what's going on?" I asked. "Where's Mom?"

He lifted his head to look at me, and I knew.

Not robbed. Abandoned.

It was Blair who pulled me into the sanctuary of my bedroom. Blair who sat on my bed while I cursed myself for buying jeans, goddamn jeans, while my mother had been—what? Loading a moving van she must have reserved in advance? Which meant she'd planned it.

Denim, it turned out, cannot be ripped apart with bare hands.

"She knew!" I screamed as I reached for the scissors on my desk. "She said good-bye to me this morning like it was any other day."

Jeans in one hand, scissors in the other, I stood in the middle of my bedroom, a shaking statue.

"Do it," Blair said. "Stab the fuck out of them. Let it out, El."

So I did, like I was Norman fucking Bates and Mom was simply taking a shower. And when it was over, when the first bout of rage had washed down the drain, I spun in a circle, lost in the emptiness created by my mother's abandonment. My ears buzzed. My body was numb. I probably would have fallen to the ground, but Blair guided me to the bed where I sat. I remember the soft give of the mattress beneath me, the relief when my legs no longer had to support me. Blair sat beside me, and I remember that as well. The warmth of her body, her hand guiding my head onto her shoulder, her mouth whispering into my hair. "Shush, shush, shush."

I remember closing my eyes and following Blair's voice back to a place where I was not alone. I don't remember her lying down on the bed or pulling me beside her. I don't remember who kissed whom first. In the year that followed, we used to tease each other about that.

Don't forget, you kissed me first. Blair would taunt.

No, I didn't, I'd insist. *You kissed me first.*

Flirtation? Foreplay? It was always the first and, more often than not, the second.

I'll never forget what followed the first kiss, whoever initiated it.

"Maybe they're not ruined," Blair said, glancing at the assaulted jeans that lay on the floor in a crumpled heap. "Why don't you put them on and we'll see?"

So I stood and took off my pants. I was about to step into the waste of one hundred and sixty dollars when Blair stopped me.

"Your underwear, too."

I looked at her like she was crazy, but she smiled at me from my bed with lips still warm and swollen from my kisses and it was impossible to deny her anything.

It was the first time I let Blair see me like that, the first time I'd let any girl see me like that, and I thought I was going to die of embarrassment. But then she smiled at me again and made it okay. I stepped into those shredded jeans and pulled them on. More than once my toes caught in the rips and I was certain I was going to topple over, but I didn't and eventually I stood in front of Blair with every one of my wounds displayed on the outside.

"Holy shit, El," she said. "You're sexy as hell in those peekaboo jeans."

"You think?" I looked in the mirror and saw what she saw. The gash that traced the curve of my ass. The rip that exposed the definition of my right thigh muscles. I saw my softness, my strength, and the vulnerable combination I'd never allowed anyone to see before. Not even me.

"Get over here," Blair practically growled. "I'll prove it." Which she did by stripping the jeans off me, and this time, when she looked at me—all of me—I felt no shame. Not that day, and not throughout the year that followed.

Until the day she punctured me, too.

Fuck Blair.

I glance at the clock. Shit, it's six o'clock. How much time have I wasted thinking about Blair? Too long. Way too long. I ditch my underwear and pull the jeans over my ass. They're scratchy. Like my skin is somehow more tender than the last time I wore them, but I ignore the feeling and flip through the hangers in my closet. I spot a gray tank top, the one with the saying across the boobs *I can't even think straight.* Perfect. And though it's Minnesota-friggin'-winter, I grab my black leather jacket, a choice based more on being cool than staying warm.

Which leaves the dilemma of my hair. A little gel manages to make those spikes look intentional. Maybe even a little badass. I throw on my favorite pair of black biker boots, add a touch of lip gloss, some killer eyeliner, and call it good enough.

I don't do purses. Ever. So I grab my keys and wallet off my dresser and shove them in my jacket pocket where I find the crumpled, but still legible, receipt for the diamond earrings. I stare at the dollar amount. One thousand three hundred and twenty-four dollars. At the time I thought it was what Blair wanted. Of course, at the time I thought *I* was what Blair wanted.

I toss the receipt on my nightstand next to the earrings. Now that I've found it, I'll be heading to the Duluth mall again, but not tonight.

Tonight I've got a date with Kate Moreau.

CHAPTER FOURTEEN

My Toyota Corolla has bucket seats, so I pick Kate up first. No way am I risking Jack calling shotgun. Besides, I need to break the news to Kate.

"Don't be mad," I tell her when she settles in beside me. Probably should have started with, *Hello, beautiful*, but I don't. I back out of the parking lot at Kate's apartment building and navigate the roads toward Jack's house.

"Why would I be mad?"

I take a quick sideways glance and see Kate looking at me, one eyebrow raised. I turn my attention back to the road and away from Kate's penetrating eyes.

"We're going to a nightclub in Duluth." I pull up in front of Jack's house.

"Really?" She smiles and then she notices I've parked my car. "Duluth is an hour away. What's up?"

The knot in my stomach tightens. "The thing is, Jack's cousin works the door at the nightclub so she'll let us in." I give the signature three quick taps of the horn and Jack emerges from the front door.

"You've got to be kidding." Kate stares at Jack as she walks down her snowy driveway toward my car.

I reach out and hold her hand. "I wanted to take you somewhere special for our second date, Kate."

"You mean our first date," she corrects me, but she doesn't pull her hand away.

"No." I touch each ring on her fingers until she smiles and I know she's remembering, too. "I mean our second date."

Kate slips her hand in mine and it feels good. So good.

Until a loud rap on the window shocks Kate and she jumps, pulling her hand out of mine. Fucking Jack, telling me to open my door, flip my driver's seat forward, and let her climb into the back. I'd let her ass freeze out there if I didn't need her to get Kate and me into Pandora's Box.

"Hello, ladies!" Jack says once she's settled into the backseat. "Ready for our double date?"

Kate turns to look at the empty seat beside Jack. "I'm sorry, did you say double date?"

Jack laughs. "Oh, it will be before the night is over. I'm gonna bust open Pandora's Box and grab the first babe to come out."

"Pandora's box?" Kate asks.

"That's the name of the club," I tell her.

Kate smiles. "I see. Are you sure that's wise, Jack? Mythologically speaking, that is."

Jack attempts to defend herself. "Well, yeah, why would I wait for the leftovers?"

Kate scowls. Probably at the concept that any woman could be a *leftover*, and I grin. Jack, who takes for granted her ability to win in any contest involving wits or words, doesn't have the first clue she's about to have her ass spanked, and hard.

"Because Pandora's box contained all the evils in the world. Clearly, a misogynistic interpretation of the myth," Kate says and I glance at Jack's reflection in the rearview mirror. She mouths the word *misogowhat?* at me and I mouth back *dicks over chicks*. Jack winks and gives me the thumbs up.

"Who could have a problem with Pandora's *box*?" I'm pretty sure if I look in the mirror again I'm going to catch Jack staring at her crotch. Pass. I'll keep my eyes on the road. "Did I ever tell you how I got my nickname?" Jack asks. "Because I'm so good at getting into—"

"Trouble?" Kate blows right past Jack's attempts to impress her. "The box, according to mythology, was actually a jar and when Pandora opened it she released evil into the world, leaving only Hope inside. So, about that dating strategy?"

Is that an awkward pause I hear in the backseat? Yep, it is, and I'm loving it.

"It was more of a hooking-up strategy," Jack finally says.

Kate shakes her head and squeezes my hand. I wish it was a speaking-of-hooking-up squeeze, but it's probably a can-you-believe-this-girl? squeeze. I probably should feel bad for Jack, because I know she's not up to Kate's sparring, but I don't. Not with Kate's hand in mine.

Kate sighs a long-suffering sigh, but I know she's having the time of her life. "What I'm suggesting is that you don't go after the first girl you meet at Pandora's Box."

From the backseat I hear Jack's voice, unusually crisp, say, "Actually, among the evils was Mischief, at least according to Hesiod, which sounds a hell of a lot hotter than Hope if you ask me."

Wow. Kate's done the impossible by getting Jack to show she's as smart as she is a smart-ass. Kate's fingers clench on mine for a second in surprise, and I cruise all the way to Duluth with her hand in mine and the hope that the night will bring more surprises.

❖

We reach Pandora's Box around eight p.m. where an older version of Jack sits on a stool inside the entrance, checking ID's and stamping women's hands. She's dark, like Jack. Thick around the middle, like Jack. And butcher than butch, also like Jack. Some women get a quick glance and stamp. Others get the whole body-scanning, hand-holding treatment. Yeah, the resemblance between Jack and her cousin is unmistakable.

"Jackamo Road!" She flashes a smile and hops off the stool to greet us. "How you doing?"

"Down and out in paradise," Jack says to her cousin. "Fact is, I need a lover."

What the—? The Jack I know may feel that way, but the Jack I also know would never, not in a million years, talk about it. She'd simply do something about it.

Jack's cousin leans toward us, filling the air with the stench of stale cigarette smoke. "Let it all hang out," she says. "Tell me how you're doing."

"Same as always," Jack says. "Between a laugh and a tear."

I stare at Jack. Sure enough, she's still Jack…on the outside, at least.

"Brilliant." Kate laughs. "Absolutely brilliant."

I stare at Kate, the question *What the hell is going on and why is it brilliant?* written all over my face, but she gives me nothing but a grin. An unreadable grin.

Jack's cousin quick-stamps the back of Jack's hand. "Don't you worry none, Jackamo. You ain't even done with the night." She stamps my hand, then smiles at Kate with a mouth full of yellow-brown teeth. "And what has you coming down the road, my sweet love?" She holds Kate's hand while she stamps it. Way too long, in my opinion.

"A little night dancin'." Kate laughs like the stamp tickles, though I know it doesn't.

"Ah, well-done. Farewell, Angelina."

"Her name is Kate," I tell Jack's cousin. "And she's with me." I loop my arm through Kate's and tug her out of Jack's cousin's clutches and into Pandora's Box, where Jack and Kate dissolve into laughter. Inexplicable, insane fits of laughter.

"That was awesome," Kate says, when she surfaces enough to gulp in a deep breath. "I may have underestimated you."

Jack bows as only Jack can bow. Deep and with much arm sweeping and without the slightest bit of humility. Meanwhile, I can draw no other conclusion than my best friend and my date have both lost their freaking minds.

"She doesn't have the first clue, does she?" Kate asks, looking at me.

Jack shakes her head. "People who listen to Tchaikovsky rarely do, but don't hold that against her."

"Oh, I won't." Kate leans toward me and her lips are cool on my flushed cheek.

"Hold what against me?" I ask, which prompts more bursts of laughter and makes me feel even more like an outsider.

The thing is, I hang out at chalets, not bars. I hover around chairlifts, not pool tables. I drink hot cocoa, sure, often spiked, but never tap beer. And yes, dammit, I do listen to Tchaikovsky and Vivaldi and Stravinsky and Debussy, not the thumping, migraine-inducing shit for music that's blasting through the speaker system.

I do not belong in Pandora's Box, though, clearly, Kate does.

"Pool!" she exclaims and walks toward the group of women who are gathered around the pool tables. Every one of them is checking Kate out as she approaches. I'd bet my ass on it. And what the hell are they doing with their pool cues? Sliding them in and out of their crooked index fingers. Blowing blue chalk dust off the tips. Eyeing Kate like she may be the easiest shot of all.

Hell, no. "Hey, Kate!" I call out to her and she turns to look at me. "Want to dance?"

She glances around the bar. "Where?"

She has a point. Pandora's Box has plenty of dartboards and pool tables and even a row of old-ass video games, but no dance floor. Not even a postage-stamp sized one. Fuck, I'd dance on a table with Kate right now if it got her away from those women.

I turn to Jack for suggestions, but she has ignored every bit of Kate's advice and taken up her post at the bar where she's making eyes at the bartender, the undoubtedly new bartender. Jack rarely goes back for seconds.

I wander over to the row of antique video game machines where it costs me a quarter to play Tetris, badly, and be confronted with the fact that I am the biggest square in the whole place. Not fitting in isn't exactly new to me, and I'd gladly pay more quarters to blend in with Ms. Pac-Man, but one of the speakers is hanging from the ceiling directly above the two of us and that migraine is quickly becoming a reality. Out of options, I plop my ass on a stool at the bar, as far away from Jack as possible, and watch Kate cue up her shot. She bends over, puts her left hand on the pool table, and balances the cue on her fingers. Far be it from me to complain about the view of her ass, but I wouldn't mind seeing her face, too. Is she biting her lower lip, the way she does when she's concentrating? Or is she glaring like she's daring the ball to defy her? She pulls the cue back, nice and slow. And then she takes the shot the way she takes a jump. Without a second of hesitation or doubt.

Crack! The cue ball strikes the head ball, scattering balls toward the sides of the table or into the pockets. Kate's voice, strong and clear, breaks through the murmurs from her admirers. "Like I always say, stroke it, ladies. Don't poke it."

This girl. This fucking girl. What have I gotten myself into? Images flood my mind of all the things I'd let Kate stroke. The temperature in the bar is suddenly, inexplicably hot, so I take off my jacket and lay it on the stool next to me.

"Compliments of Jackamo." I turn to look at the person speaking to me and find myself staring at a petite and curvy woman with electric-blue hair, placing a glass on the counter in front of me.

I take a sip and scowl. "Pepsi?" It's going to take something stronger than Pepsi for me to survive inside Pandora's Box.

"Sorry." She shrugs. "I was told you're driving tonight."

Of course I am. Kate's the kick-ass pool player. Jack's on the fast track to being the bartender's next lay. Who else would I be than the Tetris-playing, Tchaikovsky-listening, designated driver? I take another sip of my Pepsi and turn to demand a shot of whiskey, but the bartender has already returned to Jack, ready to serve up whatever she wants, by the look of it.

I sense a person standing behind me, but it's a bar, a crowded bar, so I don't give it much thought until hot breath hits the back of my neck and a voice rumbles in my ear. "Can't even think straight, huh?"

It takes a few seconds before my brain figures out what the voice is talking about. Some woman, some strange woman, has been reading the words written across my boobs from across the bar.

A hand runs from the base of my neck over the curve of my back to the patch of bare skin between my tank top and my peekaboo sexy jeans. It's a fire touch and I jerk away.

"Kate," I say and in my mind at least it sounds like a shout for help.

"Nice to meet you, Kate." A twentysomething woman in a tight black shirt and jeans moves my jacket over one stool and sits next to me. "I'm Alex."

She swivels her seat until she's facing me, and yeah, she's hot, but in an asymmetrical hairstyle and tattooed sort of way. Not my type. "I'm going to buy you a drink." Alex plants her hand on my arm the way astronauts put flags on the moon.

Not if you were the only other lesbian on the planet and all the batteries were dead, I want to say.

What I do is avoid Alex's eyes by looking anywhere else. At the older crowd out on dates with their partners; they're cozied up around tables for two and are drinking each other in with their eyes. At the other twentysomethings like Alex, looking to hook up and working it hard, hoping to score with some idiot stupid enough to waltz into Pandora's Box practically wearing a hit-on-me billboard for a tank top.

What the fuck was I thinking?

Alex runs her hand up and down my arm again. I glance over at Kate, but she's exiled two more balls into the oblivion of the pocket and she's celebrating, fitting right in with the looking-to-hook-up crowd. "Thanks, but—"

"No buts." Alex squeezes my arm and my skin rises up in gooseflesh. "What are you drinking?"

"Pepsi." I mumble something stupid about being the designated driver while trying to take out the redhead high-fiving Kate with laser beams from my eyes. The bitch.

"Pepsi?" Alex snorts, clearly disappointed in me. "We're upgrading you to a rum and Coke. Bartender!" She shouts in the direction of Jack's next conquest and holds up two fingers. "Rum and Coke," she says, "for me and my girl."

Alex leans forward and sighs. Runs her hand over my cheek. "Anyone ever told you how soft your skin is?"

"Look, Alex," I begin to say, but then two arms from behind me come out of nowhere and wrap around my body. One circles my waist while the other aims higher and ends with one of my boobs being squeezed, and for a moment I'm not sure what I should do. Turn and punch or stand and run, but then I feel her lips on my neck. Hear her voice in my ear.

"Don't worry, El. I've got you," she says. Soft, so soft.

The arms release me and then Kate steps in front of Alex and me.

"Thanks for keeping my girlfriend company while I played pool," Kate tells Alex, and then she sits on my lap and plants one on me, a kiss to end all kisses. Which, due to the human body's need for oxygen, ends eventually, and when it does I discover that Kate and I are alone in Pandora's Box.

At least that's how it feels to me.

"Miss me?" She smiles into my eyes.

More than anything, I'd tell her, if this wasn't all make-believe, but it is so I ask her a question instead. "After everything else escaped Pandora's box, what did you say she found left inside?"

"Pandora's *jar*," Kate says because she is, after all, still Kate. "And what she found was Hope."

"That's right." I put my arms around her and pull her close.

"Do you want to get out of here?" she says, which is the second-best thing I've heard all night.

"Absolutely, but there's something I have to do first."

Kate raises an eyebrow as I hop off my stool and walk over to Jack. She turns when I tap her shoulder.

"What are you doing, El?" She head-bobs in the direction of the blue-haired bartender standing a few feet from us, mixing and shaking and squirting limes into a margarita. "I'm about to close the deal."

"Trust me." I yank Jack off her stool and practically haul her to where Kate and Alex are awkwardly staring at each other.

"Alex, meet Jack." I pick up my coat and put it on, conveniently clearing my seat for the next occupant. "Jack, meet Alex."

"Nice ink," Jack says as she slides onto the stool. "I'm a bit of an aficionado." She rolls up her sleeves and the two of them start comparing tattoos.

My work here is done, but Kate's is not. She leans over and whispers something I can't hear in Jack's ear, but Jack's response is all I need to figure it out.

"Yeah, yeah, so you were right. I'll buy you a friggin' jar-shaped trophy. *Later*," Jack says, which both Kate and I take as our cue to leave.

We stumble into the lobby of Pandora's Box, not because we're drunk but because we can't stop laughing. Jack's cousin waves good-bye and blows a kiss "to Angelina," which Kate pretends to swoon over.

"Now what?" I ask, when we step onto the sidewalk. It's started to snow, light little flakes that swirl down from the sky and land on Kate's hair. As if she needed anything to make her look more beautiful.

"I suppose we have to wait for Jack," Kate says, but she's wrong. Jack will be riding tonight, but it won't be home with us to Lutsen.

"No need," I tell her and Kate doesn't ask for more details. "The night is ours. You hungry?"

"Not really. You?"

"Starving," I say. "But not for food."

Kate laughs. "You're going to have to do better than recycle a pickup line with me."

So I do. It's nine o'clock. Way too early for our date to end. If it were summer I could walk with Kate to Canal Park and show her the lift bridge and we could watch freighters enter the harbor and I could buy her popcorn from the stand and we could feed the seagulls, but it's not summer. It's a freezing cold January night.

"What now?" Kate asks, looping her arm through mine. Her gaze wanders toward Grandma's Saloon and Grill, Duluth's most famous restaurant that started off as a brothel in the nineteenth century and now hosts an annual marathon.

"Back to your place?" I suggest. The plans I have for the remainder of my date with Kate may be equally naughty and require every bit as much endurance, but they don't have a damn thing to do with the two of us sitting across from each other in a booth at some tourist trap. Not even close.

"Okay." She looks disappointed as she gets into my car, but I squelch the urge to promise her she won't be for long.

CHAPTER FIFTEEN

Y ou called me girlfriend." My voice is full of singsong
smugness as I blow past the scenic view exit and stick
to Highway 61. It's nice, riding back to Lutsen with no one and
nothing in the car but Kate, me, and the word girlfriend between
us.

"I was simply coming to your rescue," Kate says, which is too
lame an excuse to let pass.

"Uh-huh, keep telling yourself that." I grin in the darkness
illuminated only by the light from my dashboard. "Besides, who
said I needed rescuing? I was having a wonderful time with Alex.
She was admiring my soft skin."

"I bet she was." Kate throws her words the way Gordon
Ramsey throws plates of food.

"And I was admiring her tattoos."

Kate snorts, then turns to stare at me. "Wait, how did she
know your skin is soft?"

Bingo. There's the question I meant to plant in her mind. "I
suppose she noticed my soft skin when she touched me."

It's a fine moment, a glorious moment, inside the dead-silent
car as Kate figures out how much she doesn't like another woman
touching me.

"If you were having such a good time with Alex, why did you
introduce her to Jack?"

"Because Jack deserves to hit on the second hottest girl in the bar."

"I see," Kate says, "but she's not allowed to hit on the hottest girl?"

"Not if she wants to continue to be my best friend."

Kate smiles and reaches for my hand, and yeah, it's a line straight out of The Blair Bitch Project.

I turn on the radio, but when the sound of wailing strings and clashing cymbals comes out of the car's speakers, Kate starts hitting the preset buttons. They're all more of the same, so she eventually gives up, turns off the radio, and we ride the rest of the way home in the type of silence that asks too many questions for anyone to be comfortable.

It's only ten o'clock when I pull up in front of Kate's apartment, but I'll be damned if I know how to invite myself in so we can continue our date. I need Maggie. And maybe some squash. But neither seems likely.

Kate reaches for the handle and I'm resigning myself to the fact that I've probably blown our date when she stops and turns toward me. "If I was the hottest girl in the bar, why didn't you play pool with me? Why did you spend the whole night at the bar with Alex?"

"Because…" Shit. I don't know how to explain it. "I've never played pool. Not even once."

She releases the door handle. "So?"

"So I didn't want to make a fool of myself in front of you."

She laughs, but it's clear she's picturing me at the bar with Alex. "How'd that work out for you?"

"Not bad," I tell her, truthfully. "It got you to kiss me, didn't it?"

And then Kate blows me away. "If you want me to kiss you, all you have to do is ask," she says. No way did I see that coming and no way am I missing an opportunity like this. Not when she's made the offer and there's no taking it back.

"I want you to kiss me," I say and she closes her eyes. I could kiss her. Right then and there...if I could only figure out how to navigate the stupid stick shift and the seat belts and the goddamn bucket seats and the armrests between us. "Fuck!"

Kate's eyes fly open. "What? What's wrong?"

"I want to kiss you, but not like this. Not here."

She turns away from me and the door pings. A blast of cold air floods the car. She swings one foot out of the door and then the other. She's halfway out of the car before my mouth and mind reconnect.

"You're leaving? Just like that?" This is not how our date is supposed to end. I reach for her arm, but Kate is moving so fast she slips through my fingers and is outside in the snow before I know it.

She leans inside the car to look at me. "Are you coming inside with me or what?"

Which is precisely how I hoped our date would end, so I climb out of the car and walk with Kate up the sidewalk to her apartment building. The hallway still smells of dirty diapers and fried onions and I really hate that she lives here, but where anyone lives is beyond my control.

We stand on the *Nice Underwear* doormat as Kate slides the key into the lock and opens the door. Turd Ferguson, of course, is right there to announce our arrival with a deep growl, and I damn near have a heart attack on the spot.

"Shush, Turd! Be quiet!" I pick the dog up, which stops her growling but jumpstarts her licking.

"Knock it off, Turd. Ellie's my date tonight," Kate says and I start to feel good about the direction the night is taking.

We walk through the dark apartment in a row. First Kate, then me, and finally Turd, traipsing through the living room and down the hallway, until we reach the room I'm almost positive is Maggie's bedroom.

"What about your mom?" I whisper, like we're about to get busted for breaking and entering. Make that unlatching and snatching.

Kate looks at me like she doesn't get the question. "What about her?"

"What would she say?" I nod toward Kate's bedroom door. "About what we're going to do."

Kate raises an eyebrow. "And what is it you think we're going to do?"

Well, first I thought I'd take your shirt off and then you'd... Yeah, right. Like I'm going to stand outside her mom's room talking about my visions of rebound sex with Kate.

"I thought we were going to..." I stand there, probably blushing like a freaking stop sign again at the thought of Kate's hands on my body. "You know."

She places one finger on my chest. One. And not even anywhere near the fun places. "You assume too much." She puts some power behind that one finger until I'm backed up against the wall and staring at the door to Maggie's bedroom. "And as for what my mom would say..." Kate removes her finger from my chest and runs her hand over her face to push away a nonexistent flop of hair. She drops the pitch of her voice. "You two are perfect for each other, that's for damn sure."

It's a spot-on Maggie imitation and I can't help but laugh.

Maggie can't either. "Hello, girls," she says from behind the closed door. "Did you two have fun on your date?"

"Don't know yet, Mom. It's not over," Kate says like it's no big deal Maggie knows we're continuing our date inside Kate's bedroom.

I consider what my mom would say. If she were around to say anything, that is.

"Okay. 'Night, girls." The bed squeaks and I imagine Maggie rolling over and settling back into sleep.

What the fuck? I mouth the words to Kate who holds up a finger.

"Wait for it," she whispers, her shoulders shaking with laughter she's trying to keep quiet.

"Oh, and Eleanor?" Maggie's voice comes through the door again and grabs me by my gonads.

"Yes, ma'am?" My voice comes out squeakier than shit, but Maggie called me Eleanor *and* caught me trying to sneak into her daughter's bedroom.

"Do not, under any circumstance, disrespect my daughter," Maggie says and I can hear the don't-piss-off-the-mother edge in her voice. "Understand?"

"Yes, ma'am." *Yes, ma'am. Yes, ma'am.* I'm a freaking broken record stuck on repeat and playing "The Star Spangled Banner."

"Good. Then you're welcome here." I swear I can feel Maggie's grip on my gonads loosen. "Until midnight when your ass better be out that door and making its way back home. Got it?"

"Yes, ma'am," I say again and this time Kate doesn't even try to silence her laughter as she opens her bedroom door and pulls me inside.

"Yes, ma'am?" She doubles over, gripping her stomach and hiccuping with laughter.

Not exactly the pose I had in mind for her.

"Oh, shut up," I say as I cross the room to sit on her bed and sulk. Turd jumps up beside me, puts her head on my lap, and stares at me with those milk-chocolate eyes. At least I'm getting love from someone.

Kate hits the wall switch and kills the overhead lighting. I use the cover of darkness to wipe off as much dog drool with my tank top as possible while Kate makes her way to her desk and turns on a small paper lamp that spins and throws tiny lights, like stars, on the walls and ceiling. It casts the room in a soft glow so when Kate sits next to me on the bed everything will be perfectly romantic.

If it weren't for the stench of dog breath rising up between us.

Kate picks up Turd and drops her gently to the floor. "Go lie in your bed," she says, and Turd miraculously obeys.

"Kate, I want you to—"

"Dance naked?" she asks, a half smile playing at the corner of her lips.

I like to think I field surprises pretty well, but that one hits me like whiplash. "Ah, I…sure. Yeah. Great."

"Okay. You got it." Kate stands and my heart feels like it's going to beat out of my chest. My mouth is surprisingly dry. Other parts of me, predictably damp. She walks to the middle of her bedroom and turns to look at me.

"You ready for a wild night?" she asks, and even in the soft light I can see her eyes sparkling with the delight she gets out of torturing me.

I can't even talk so I nod. And wait. And watch. And hold my breath.

She pulls her phone out of her pocket and plugs a cord into the AV jack on her nightstand. She swipes the phone with her finger until her apps show.

"Pandora," she says. "Gotta love it." For a minute I think she's talking about that awful bar, but then music plays through speakers propped on the headboard of her bed and I realize she's setting the mood for her striptease with the music app, Pandora. Fine by me, Katie girl.

I'm ready. More than ready. Actually, I'm fairly freaked out but still ready.

And then she lies down on the bed and closes her eyes.

The fuck?

"I'm confused. Didn't you say you were going to dance naked, because I'm pretty sure I heard something about you and dancing and being naked?" I'm rambling when Kate reaches up, grabs the back of my tank top, and pulls me onto the bed beside her.

"Shut the fuck up and listen," she says, so I do.

And I hear music like no music I've heard before. The song opens with street noise, a car horn honking, two beeps, and then a guitar intro followed by a man singing with a voice full of smoke and broken mirrors.

Kate lies on her back, listening. I lean on my side, watching Kate listen, and I see the music when it crawls beneath her skin and moves her from the inside. I witness her "Dance Naked" on a "Wild Night," and I count the times her chest rises and falls as she chuckles through "Jackamo Road," and when "Farewell Angelina" plays, I lean close and hear her whisper every single word.

"Do you hear it, Ellie?" she asks me, her eyes still closed. "How good a thing can be when it's honest?"

"Yeah, I think so. Maybe," I say, but then "I Need a Lover" begins to play and no way am I ready to face the truth in that song so I reach across Kate's body and put Pandora on pause.

John Mellencamp, I read. There's one name I won't forget.

Kate turns to me with eyes full of *Now's your chance so don't blow it.* "Wasn't there something you wanted to ask me?"

I don't know if it's Maggie's words—*don't disrespect my daughter*—or the truth laid bare by John Mellencamp, but I can't, I can't, I can't ask Kate to kiss me. Not if the whole point of the Kate and Ellie rematch is for me to get over Blair. If I knew for a fact there was more, something real between us, then maybe I could, but I don't know that any more than I know what to say to Kate when she looks at me, waiting for me to ask her a question. *The* question.

I grab at the first safe thought to flit through my head. "Who taught you to play pool like that?"

Kate blinks. "My dad."

"Yeah? That's cool." I breathe a sigh of relief when she turns her head to stare at the ceiling and the spinning spots of light. "Where does he live?"

"No clue," Kate says. "But he's out there somewhere, placing his next bet. Winning some. Losing more. Probably in Vegas. That's where Mom says all gambling addicts go to die."

Her voice is full of dying embers and broken promises and I feel it creep beneath my skin and move me from the inside. "John Mellencamp should write a song about that," I tell her.

"He did. 'Gambling Bar Blues,'" she says with a smile, a very sad smile.

"So it's life according to John Mellencamp for you, huh?"

She nods. "Better than Tchaikovsky. Who told you that was good music?"

Fair enough.

"My mom," I answer her. "She's a violinist."

"I haven't met her yet," Kate says.

If my answer were a Mellencamp song it would be full of fire and the broken pieces of a family my mother threw away. Maybe Kate can live life according to Mellencamp, but I can't.

"She travels a lot with the orchestra. You'll meet her soon," I tell her. What I don't tell her is that soon will happen the day the Boston Philharmonic moves to Minnesota. "I'm sorry your dad left you. That has to hurt."

Kate snuggles into me, weaving one leg between mine. She turns her face to me, her eyes already half closed and I know what she wants, but damn, my heart's pounding so fast Kate has to feel it and I can't. I can't. Not like this either. Not with the taste of another lie in my mouth.

I hold Kate for I don't know how long. Probably past Maggie's deadline of midnight, but the idea that either of us has to obey some arbitrary parental curfew feels laughable. I stare at the lights that fall on the posters above Kate's bed. It's the closest she's ever gotten to seeing the real night sky at those ski resorts, and it isn't fair. Not even close. Kate traces the ragged tears in my jeans. She even says they remind her of how easy it is to be ripped apart, and she's right. Tonight, I know, is the last time I'll wear these jeans because Blair was wrong. There's nothing peekaboo sexy about pain.

I do eventually kiss Kate. I kiss her eyelids when she closes them because she can't let me look into her any longer and I kiss her hair when she rests her head on my shoulder. But I do not ask Kate to kiss me. And I do not tell Kate about my mother.

I will.

Someday. When it's right.

If I can ever remember what right feels like.

Chapter Sixteen

Dear Mom,
Have you heard of John Mellencamp? If not, you
should listen to him.
By the way, you suck.
E.

This is the letter I write to Irina Engebretsen, c/o the Boston Philharmonic. I write it because truth demands a voice. I even mail it, but two weeks later, with no response, I face the fact that sometimes giving truth a voice doesn't change a damn thing.

Mom is still in Boston, presumably chasing her dream and Bernard.

Dad is still in Minnesota, counting down the days until Utah and trying to pretend his heart isn't breaking.

And Kate and I are still training our asses off.

When the International Continental Cup is three weeks away, Kate and I step it up even more. We hit the exercise room before Kate goes to school and stay two hours past the regular Lab Rat practices. On Saturdays and Sundays, we jump. Sometimes a dozen, two dozen times per day. It's a grueling pace, but I know—even if Kate doesn't—that she can only fly so far on natural talent and raw guts.

A lot of things feel different since Pandora's Box. For one, there's a whole lot more touching between Kate and me. In the exercise room. In her bedroom. Sometimes, even in mine when Dad isn't skulking around the place. It's never like the night in the hotel though, when anything was possible because nothing mattered. It's mostly PG-13. Sometimes NC-17. Regardless of the rating, it's flirty, uncertain, awkward as fuck, and I have no idea why. I mean, I'm only dating Kate to help me get over Blair, right?

Right...?

So why the hell do I feel jittery around her all the time?

Except, that is, when we're in the exercise room. There, I lead and she follows. I say jump hurdles, Kate jumps hurdles. I say land on a moving board, Kate lands on a moving board. And when she's got that down, I add ankle weights. At the two-week-precompetition point, I dig into Dad's equipment cupboard, pull out the board swing, and attach it to the hooks in the ceiling.

"Now what are you doing to me?" Kate eyes the one-by-three-foot board swinging back and forth.

"That's a question for the bedroom," I remind her. "Not here."

"Fuck you," she says, though there's more offer than offense in her voice, and I'd take her up on it if I thought Kate's vertical spring could be improved horizontally.

"It's easy, Kate. Take the hurdles like usual but after you clear the last one, ride the board until you reach the swing, jump off, and land on it."

Kate looks at her weighted ankles, the board, the hurdles, the swing, then back to me. It's a long and scathing look.

"Without falling," I add.

"Impossible," she says. "No one can do that."

"Wanna bet?" I ask, but Kate's too smart to fall for that twice.

By the end of the week she clears all five hurdles, jumps, lands on the swing, and it's official. She's as ready for the International Continental Cup as she's going to be.

But I'm not.

There's still one hurdle I've got to clear before Kate and I can fly off to Utah.

❖

The mall is quiet post-Christmas. Gone are the bell ringers outside the mall doors and the obnoxious kids wailing in line to meet fake Santas. It's even possible to walk down the hall to the jewelry store without feeling like a salmon swimming upstream.

"Can I help you?" a middle-aged man in a pinstripe suit and a red power tie asks me when I put the small black box on the glass cabinet.

"I'd like to return these." I dig the crumpled receipt out of my pocket and hand it to him.

He opens the lid on the box and looks at the one-carat diamond earrings glittering in the fluorescent light, then at me. More precisely, at my boobs. "Now why would a pretty little girl like you want to return these?"

I glance at his name tag, but it's wrong. Douglas Jenkins? No way. This dude's name is Richard, Dick for short. His middle name is Peter and his last name's gotta be Johnson. No way this douchebag is named Douglas Jenkins.

"I think you've misunderstood," I tell Dick Peter Johnson. "They weren't a gift for me. In fact, I bought them for my girlfriend for Christmas."

He blinks. Twice. It's the word girlfriend coming out of another girl's mouth.

"Oh, I see. Didn't she like them?" He flinches and grasps for his fragile masculinity before it slips away from him completely, which is when I know it's time to have some fun.

I crank the volume of my voice up one notch. "Don't know. She dumped me a week before Christmas for someone with a penis, so you see why I'm returning them, don't you?"

"Of course. Yes, of course, I do." The salesman glances around the store. "I assume crediting your card would be fine?"

So, so fine.

Almost as fine as watching a homophobe's bluster turn into fluster. Almost as fine as walking out of the mall with one thousand three hundred and twenty-four dollars back in my bank account. Almost as fine as knowing that Kate's trip to Utah is covered.

I give Dad the cash and tell him it's from Kate. I have to lie because he'd hit the roof if he knew I spent my savings on sending her to Utah. He would have lost it if he'd found out about the diamond earrings I bought for Blair, too, but I wasn't worried then, and I'm not worried now. By the time Dad discovers my empty bank account, I'll have endorsement money. Plenty of it. So I hand over every penny I have and tell him it's from Kate, and it's by far the easiest lie I've told so far.

What's not so easy is trying to convince Kate and Maggie over dinner that evening that the cost for Utah is covered by the Gravity Lab tuition Kate's working off in the pro shop. Kate doesn't question it, but Maggie comes up with an excuse to grill me after dinner.

"Kate, is Turd sitting by the door? Will you take her out please? Oh, and Ellie, would you give me a hand with the dishes?"

Kate and Turd aren't two steps out of the apartment when Maggie pulls me into the kitchen and shoves a drying cloth in my hands.

"I've been all over the country," Maggie says as she squirts dish soap into the sink of warm water. "Want to know the one thing I've found to always be true?"

Bubbles rise up in the water. Maggie slides the dinner plates into the sink where they *thunk* against each other. She plucks one out, wipes it clean, and holds it under the stream of water until all the soap bubbles wash away.

"You should always travel with paper plates?" I take the slippery plate from Maggie and dry it with the towel. I get lucky when I correctly choose the cabinet where Maggie keeps the plates—a wild guess.

She keeps talking while I put the plate away. "No. The one universal truth everywhere is there's no such thing as a free meal." She plunges her hands back into the sink and comes up with a delicate bowl covered in ivy vines and roses to wash and rinse. "You can sell Kate your bogus tuition story because she wants to go to Utah so bad she'll buy it, but that's not going to work on me. I want to know the truth, Ellie. Who paid for my daughter's trip to Utah?"

My plan is to stick to the tuition story, but the bowl is so wet and slippery, I drop it on the floor.

"I'm so sorry!" I bend down to pick up the assorted pieces that were her bowl seconds ago. "Can I replace it? Where did you buy it?"

Maggie shakes her head. "That design is no longer made. It was from my mother's wedding dishes."

The fragments of the bowl bite into my hands like thorns on a rose. "I am so sorry."

"It's fine," Maggie takes the broken pieces from me and places them on the counter. "It was an accident. I would, however, like an answer to my question. Who paid for my daughter's trip to Utah?"

There's no way I can lie to Maggie now.

"I did," I tell her. "Out of my savings." The front doorknob begins to turn and I have to blurt out the most important part. "Please don't tell Kate. She'd never go if she knew."

Maggie smiles and pats me on the cheek. "You're starting to figure out my daughter. Good for you, Ellie Bean, and don't worry about the bowl."

Unfortunately, Kate hears Maggie call me Ellie Bean, which she pounces on the way Harry the hairy cat pounces on Turd Ferguson. She even tries it out at Lab Rat practice later that week, but I shut her up by calling her CupKate and making lewd references to having my cake and eating it, too.

After that fiasco we go back to calling each other El and Kate. Sometimes I think about calling Kate my girlfriend, but I don't. Not because it doesn't feel right, but because it *does*. And that was never the plan, so I don't have a fucking clue how to feel about it.

On Wednesday, two days before we're supposed to leave for Utah, Kate and I cut training short to crash at her place. Maggie, as far as I know, has kept my secret and spent every spare minute away from Flex Appeal washing and packing Kate's clothes. I don't have the heart to tell her Kate doesn't own one suitable thing for a ski jumping competition. Instead I help Maggie fold Kate's clothes and put them into her suitcase, and later, with Dad's begrudging blessing, I raid the pro shop and pack a second suitcase, one filled with all the necessary gear in precisely Kate's size.

Some secrets, I figure, Maggie doesn't need to know.

CHAPTER SEVENTEEN

Somewhere about 35,000 feet above Wyoming, Kate takes out her earbuds and turns to me. "Tell me I'm not dreaming, El."

"You're not dreaming," I say for the third time since takeoff.

"I must be," she's says, fiddling with her iPod. "This isn't my life."

I turn to Dad, who got the aisle seat whether he wanted it or not. "Tell her she's not dreaming."

Dad leans across me and talks to Kate. "I hate to break it to you, but you're right. This isn't your life. Not the life you knew anyway. But this is the life you'd better get used to because you're great. You hear me? You're a great jumper."

Kate's eyes tear up, and she's so beautiful that looking at her is like staring into the sun. Damn near blinding. "I wouldn't even be here if it wasn't for you and Ellie," Kate says. "I don't know how to thank you."

"Coaching someone who was born to jump is thanks enough," Dad says.

I'm sandwiched between a lovefest and I don't mind one bit until Blair and Geoffrey-with-a-*G*, in the row behind me, start making slurpy kissing sounds. I get ready to cringe, but then I realize I don't feel it. The stab at the thought of her with him. The gut twist at the image of him inside her. Sure, there's still a pinch, but who cringes when they're pinched, especially when they're sitting next to a beautiful girl?

Kate has returned to staring out her window, her head bobbing, which doesn't make any sense until I see she's put her earphones in and is flying high, probably with John Mellencamp.

"Thanks," I tell Dad and he pats my arm. In Peder Engebretsen-speak, that's the equivalent of a giant bear hug that lifts me off the ground and twirls me in the air. Quite the feat, considering I can still feel agony radiating from him.

"Did you sign the papers yet?" I've been afraid to ask, but he needs to talk to someone and I'm all he's got.

"Yeah," he says. "I mailed them to her yesterday."

It's breaking the number one Engebretsen rule, ski on the surface, but I don't give a damn. He's hurting. He's pissed. And I know what that feels like. "It's her loss, Dad. You do know that, don't you?" I ask him.

Dad hunches over, rests his elbows on his knees and his forehead on the church and steeple he makes with his hands. He looks like he's praying. It's an alarming sight.

"In a divorce," he whispers. "Everybody loses."

It's a statement I'd challenge if we weren't stuck in a plane flying toward Park City, Utah, and if Dad wasn't on the verge of either a nervous breakdown or a religious conversion.

Kate, oblivious to it all, yanks her earbuds out and grabs my knee. "Look, El. We're descending through the clouds! We're almost there. We're actually going to compete in the International Continental Cup. How can we be so lucky?"

I look to my right, but all I see is Kate staring out the window with a wonder I haven't felt in years. When did I stop feeling lucky? Was it when Blair broke my heart? When Mom left? Or earlier, much earlier, when Dad's smile depended on the sum of my style points plus length of my jump?

"Yeah, we're lucky," I say, but I don't feel it deep down the way Kate does.

Beneath us something makes a sound like a dull *thunk* and Kate inhales sharply.

"It's okay," I tell her. "The pilot lowered the landing gear, that's all. You ready?"

She nods, and I almost believe her. The clouds are above us again, where they belong, and Kate looks out the window at the Wasatch Mountains and the roads that zigzag downward, all heading toward the same destination, Utah Olympic Park. She turns and looks at me, her face lit up with excitement. "Isn't it the most beautiful sight you've ever seen, El?"

I smile. My ears pop. My eyes flick from the mountains to the gleam in Kate's eyes.

Not even close, I want to tell her, but then we're touching down on planet Earth and the brakes are screeching and we're being flung off balance, and by the time we come to a full stop, the moment has passed.

Once off the plane, we head to baggage claim where Dad takes off to conquer the rent-a-van challenge, leaving Geoffrey, Blair, Kate, and me to wait for our small fortune of ski equipment to appear, preferably in working condition.

It's an awkward twenty minutes, to say the least, especially when Blair decides she absolutely needs to have a heart-to-heart with me right here, right now.

"Hey, El. Can we talk?"

Kate's hand in mine tightens. What is Blair thinking?

"You're joking, right?" I snap and she flinches. Actually flinches. But what the hell? Did she check her common sense in Minneapolis? Maybe it'll come shooting down the carousel ramp any minute and she'll remember how things stand between us.

"No joke," she says. "There's something I've been wanting to say to you for a long time."

Nope. Nope. Nope. Her common sense is speeding toward Iceland on the wrong plane. Or New Guinea. Or Zanzibar. Anywhere but Park City, Utah.

"Not interested, Blair." I entwine my fingers in Kate's. "Now why don't you go stand by your boyfriend before he bursts into tears?"

Blair glances at the sad-faced Geoffrey-with-a-*G*, then back at me, and ultimately seems to decide misery is better company than hostility. Kate doesn't make any comment on Blair's sudden intrusion, which is one of the reasons she's a great jumper. She's already mastered Dad's first lesson: *Don't create unnecessary friction*. Finally our luggage and ski equipment arrive and we reconnect with Dad who loads everything into the van.

Dad in the driver's seat and Geoffrey and Blair in the backseat are silent, but I'm talking enough for everybody. There are about one thousand and one cool things I want to tell Kate about Utah Olympic Park.

"There are six jumps. *Six!* From ten meters to one hundred twenty meters," I tell her.

"Why so many?" Kate asks.

"You want the original reason or the new reason?"

Kate doesn't bother answering because, of course, she wants all the reasons.

"Okay, the original answer is that Park City hosted the Olympics in 2002 and they built a kick-ass ski jumping park, right Dad?"

From the driver's seat, Dad chuckles. "You should know. You were there." Kate's eyes widen a titch and I'm fine with that. Until Dad spoils a perfectly good impressing-Kate moment with sentimental drivel. "Eleanor was four and she rode on my shoulders the whole time. I'll never forget how she repeated the same two words over and over during the entire ski jumping competition. *Someday, Daddy.* That's what she said. Know what, Eleanor?" He flashes a look at me in the rearview mirror. "Today is one day closer to someday."

Holy shit. Next he's going to be telling Kate I was potty-trained by eighteen months. I send him an easy to read shut-the-fuck-up look, which, thankfully, he does. "Current reason, Utah Olympic Park is the headquarters for the U.S. Ski Team as well as the Fly Girls." I pull Kate's attention back to me where it belongs. "They're a training program for girls who are into ski jumping and the best Fly Girls will have no problem making the U.S. National and Olympic Teams."

Kate scrunches her eyebrows.

"What's wrong?" I ask her, quietly.

"It's…I'm starting so late."

It hits me then. Kate's been thinking she might have a shot at the U.S. National if not the Olympic team, which is absurd. She's good. Better than good, but she's a complete unknown hitting the scene for the first time at this weekend's competition. Plus, she's about fifty cents above being broke and I'm out of diamonds so there's no chance of her catching the IOC's attention at the international competitions. But I can't break that news to her so I mumble, "Better late than never," and hope the stupid saying gives Kate some comfort.

It's a quiet ride as Dad drives the forty miles from Salt Lake City to Park City. Kate's probably feeling what I'm feeling: the gap between us. The chance I have that she'll never have. I'd reach for her hand, but something prickly in the air tells me I shouldn't.

Finally, Dad drives past a sign that reads *Utah Olympic Park, next exit* and her whole mood changes. She's Kate from the airplane again with her nose mashed against the car window. Dad takes the exit, but instead of driving us to the park, he pulls up in front of the Newpark Resort. Kate looks confused for a moment, and I realize she doesn't know there's no lodging at the park, but then something catches her attention and astonishment replaces confusion.

"Is that—?"

I glance out the van window and see two girls walking out the front door. "Sarah Hendrickson and Nita Englund? Yep. All the competitors stay in hotels in the Redstone area, but we run into each other and hang out before the competition. I'll introduce you to everyone later."

For the first time since I've known her, Kate looks intimidated.

I open the van door and step out. Kate scoots down the seat and follows me. "Don't worry," I tell her when we're outside and walking around the van to get our gear. "Off the hill, we're all friends."

"And on it?" she asks.

Dad, who has opened the back doors and is shoving suitcases at me, answers. "You're competitors."

Which is only part of the answer and if Kate is going to stop fading to gray in front of my eyes, she needs to know the most important thing about women's ski jumping.

"We're allies, more than anything," I tell her, "fighting for equality in a misogynistic sport."

Kate smiles at the word misogynistic and the memory of the trip to Pandora's Box, no doubt. Her smile leads to her taking a deep breath, and before the last suitcase hits the ground, Kate's cheeks have returned to a sexy shade of rose.

We head into the Newpark Resort and Dad checks us in as a group, then doles out key cards, which gets Kate and me laughing to everyone's bewilderment, which only makes us laugh harder. Unlike Jack's free-to-friends policy, the person working the front desk here expects guests to pay. Normally we'd bunk together to save money, but Dad took one look at the dynamics of any Blair-Ellie-Kate combination and sprang for individual rooms. At least for the girls. Geoffrey-with-a-*G* and Dad are going to be spending a cozy weekend together.

Yeah, I sort of love it when karma delivers a much-needed and long-overdue kick to the balls.

Know what's even better? When karma puts Kate and me in adjoining rooms. I drop one suitcase—mine, open my connecting door, and start knocking.

She opens her door and glances down at the suitcase in my hand. "Let me guess, your thermostat's broken or your toilet's clogged or there's a cockroach on your pillow so you have no choice but to move in to my room."

Not a bad idea at all, but not why I'm there. I cross the room and put my, make that *her*, suitcase on the bed.

"Pretty sure we'd get caught," Kate says, still not understanding.

"Why don't you just get over here? I've got a surprise for you."

Kate joins me by the bed and it's easy, so easy, to remember the last time we were alone in a hotel room, the only time we've had sex. I want to again. Here, now. So much. Too much, maybe. It's all I've been thinking about for weeks. Kate and me alone in a hotel again. But everything is different now. She's not some stranger anymore, not just a warm body. She's Kate, and that means something to me. Maybe everything to me.

"Open it," I tell her. "Before I start babbling like a sentimental idiot." I can't wait to see her face.

She grabs the zipper and pulls it around three sides, lifts the lid, and freezes.

For approximately two seconds.

Then she dives in, pulling out the best jumpsuit we carry in the pro shop, a new helmet, goggles, gloves, even a winter coat. All in her size. She puts on the red jacket with blue and white accents that practically shouts Team USA and stands there, looking at herself in the mirror. She plays with the zipper, up, down, up, then slips her hands into the pockets where she finds my note.

Tell Cassandra White to fuck off. You don't need her coat anymore.

And that's when Kate Moreau, the always strong and independent Kate Moreau, does something I never thought she'd do. She cries. Not in big, soppy, messy tears. More like a few rogue drops of happiness that slide down those sexy rose-colored cheeks of hers.

"El?"

"Yeah?"

"I don't think we're not *not* okay anymore." It's a sentence that wouldn't make sense to anyone else, but I know exactly what she's saying. The words make me feel like I could cry, too. With relief and that same delirious happiness I see in her eyes, but also because I know I don't deserve her.

How could I after using her to get over Blair? To get even with Blair? How could I have been so stupid? Thinking she was just someone, anyone, when all along she has been The One.

"Oh God, I...I..." I have to tell her everything, confess all the lies, but where do I begin? I don't have a clue. I only know I can't stand any distance between us.

Not anymore.

Evidently neither can Kate, because she's in my arms before I can find the words, and I need to touch her more than I've ever needed to touch anyone. Even Blair. Especially Blair. But lies aren't the only thing between us. There's thermodynamic material and inches and inches of down and puffy sleeves. Kate's cocooned in her jacket.

"It's beautiful, but..." She pulls it off and throws it on the bed, then throws me on the bed.

I barely feel the weight of Kate's body on top of mine. I'm too busy feeling her hands under my shirt. I do feel the crushing weight of my lies, but her mouth on mine makes it impossible to say what I should have said ages ago: I've been lying to her but also to myself. Maybe mostly to myself.

She breaks our kiss and I could tell her then, but she's moving until she's sitting on me, straddling me and reaching for the hem of her shirt. One swift movement. Up, up, and off, and I am suddenly, completely, incapable of speech.

Gone are the days when she led and I followed. Gone are the days when I worried about such things. We merge into a blur of stripping bodies. She's wriggling out of her jeans while I'm unbuttoning my shirt and then I'm kicking off my pants and hitting my head on the suitcase. I jerk sideways, more from surprise than pain. Kate tears herself away from me, lifts the suitcase, and sets it on the floor. We've been on top of the new jacket and I don't want it to stay wrinkled. I want Kate to remember this, remember us, for all sorts of reasons, but looking like she slept on her jacket isn't one of them.

I carry the jacket to the chair pushed in under the little desk across the room. Spreading it over the back of the chair, I run my hands across the shoulders, smoothing out some of the wrinkles. Kate is back in the bed. She's pulled down the blankets and when I turn around she's a long expanse of honey bare skin on the white sheets.

I want to stand there and look at her for an hour or two, even with my ass getting cold. But then she takes off her rings, setting them, one by one, on the bedside table with the crisp click of metal on wood, and I need her hands on me again.

It doesn't take long to get to where she almost makes me scream. I clench my teeth when I realize the sounds coming out of me are probably audible in the hall and Blair's nearby room, but fuck her. This isn't about Blair anymore. With a jolt, I realize it hasn't been for a long time.

I ride the waves down. Catch my breath. Find myself in a dilemma. It's her turn to lose control, but we never got that far in condo 103. I make a sweeping hand gesture down her body and hope that's clear enough. She laughs and rolls onto her back.

"Really?" I ask and she answers by putting my hand between her legs. Kate is many things. Fucking sexy. Sassy as hell. Not even a little bit subtle. God, I love that about her.

I start slow, but she says, "More."

"I don't want to hurt you," I say, and the words catch in my throat. I've done so many things without giving one thought to her pain.

"How could you?" she asks.

The answers that collect on the edges of my mind make me want to fly away. Not from Kate, but from who I've become.

I get into position and visualize the sequence of actions to make the jump last as long as possible and land well.

Blame the sport.

Kate runs her fingers through my hair. "El?" she asks and I look up at her. "Relax. Let yourself go."

Can I do that? Jump on instinct like Kate jumps?

Yes, yes, I can. With Kate, inside Kate, there is no need to rush the inrun, no points for style, no pressure to go the distance or land perfectly. There's just Kate, and me, and the two of us learning to fly together.

❖

Kate lies on the bed, each leg and arm pointing in a different direction. She's a compass. A naked and flushed, shining with sweat, hair tumbling over her face compass.

How could I not see that before?

It's as clear to me as the rise and fall of her chest.

With Kate, I can breathe. With Kate, I'll never feel lost again, and I'll never let anything endanger that. Especially not some confession that will only hurt her.

I run my fingers down the inside of her arm. "Hey, you awake?"

"No." She squirms. "Definitely not."

I run my fingers down her side and she pulls away, laughing.

"Don't make me find your ticklish spot," Kate says.

It's a game I'd gladly play with her all night, if only we could. I stand and pull clothes over skin that still throbs from her touch. "We've got to get ready."

"For what?" She groans, sits up, and leans against the bed's headboard, her body glowing in a patch of light from the window where the sun hangs low in the sky.

"Dinner." I break the news to her. "Dad insists we eat together as a team before every competition. It's a tradition and he'd blow a gasket if we missed it. In fact, they're probably all waiting for us in the lobby now."

Kate does not move. She sits there, in all her nakedness, and lets me stare at her. She doesn't hide from me and she doesn't pose for me.

"We eat," she says. "And then we go. I'm not in the mood to share you with anyone, especially…"

She doesn't have to finish. We both know how that sentence ends.

"We'll go down there, eat some steak, ignore two assholes, make the old man happy, and then we'll watch the sunset over the Wasatch Mountains. Deal?"

"Deal." She gets out of bed and walks naked to the bathroom.

Slowly.

So slowly.

I look in the mirror to see if I need to clean up before dinner, too, but what I see is someone with messed up hair aching for Kate's fingers. Someone with a ridiculous grin on her face. Someone whose head is surrounded by clouds.

Someone unable to deny what she's feeling.

Fucking happy.

In other words, someone I hardly recognize at all.

CHAPTER EIGHTEEN

Lake Superior is to Minnesota as the Wasatch mountain range is to Utah. I grew up surrounded by fir and birch and the endless expanse of blue. Nature is a show-off in Utah, too, but in a different way. The mountain range treats the small villages that nestle in its valleys the way I imagine the big brother I always wanted would treat a little sister, acting all big and tough and pompous as hell, but strong enough to help carry the load of Dad's dreams for Engebretsen gold.

Admittedly, the Wasatch mountain range has earned its bragging rights. It's the western edge of the greater Rocky Mountains and the eastern edge of the Great Basin region. It also has snow so dry and powdery it's called the greatest on earth, which is why the Wasatch mountain range is the big brother to eleven ski resorts, three of which surround Park City.

It's forty degrees outside, practically shorts weather to anyone fresh from Minnesota's minus-ten temperature, but Kate insists on wearing her new jacket as she, Dad, Blair, Geoffrey-with-a-*G*, and I head out of the hotel in search of dinner. She fidgets with it as we walk, playing with the zipper, checking out the hidden pocket for her iPod, running her hand across the slick thermodynamic fabric. She has that *I must be dreaming* look in her eyes again as we walk under the metal archway that reads REDSTONE and enter the quaint district in Park City where world-class skiers and families on vacation eat in the same restaurants and shop in the same stores.

Dad is in the lead, with Geoffrey and Blair trailing behind him. Kate and I are fine lagging far behind. Something has changed between us. Sure, she's still a kid at Disney, head rotating in every direction, eyes huge, determined not to miss a thing. But it's impossible for us to stop touching each other. She pulls her hand out of mine to point at something she can't believe she's seeing and I slip my arm around her back. Eventually her hand finds mine again and we walk forward. Exploring. Discovering. Redstone and each other.

"Oh my God." Kate stops in her tracks and is staring at a woman walking toward us.

"Hey, Ellie." The legend smiles as she nears us.

"Hey, Lindsey." I turn to introduce Kate, but she looks like she's going to faint or fangirl on the spot. "Good luck tomorrow," I say.

"You, too." Lindsey Van walks past us.

Blair, oblivious that one of the greatest jumpers of all time has stopped to talk to us, is obnoxiously pointing out the shops like we came here to buy Coach purses or Manolo Blahnik shoes. She oohs and aahs the entire walk to the Red Rock Junction restaurant while I spend the time wondering what I ever saw in her in the first place.

Besides, of course, her obvious assets.

The place is slammed, and we wait twenty minutes before it's our turn to be seated. We follow the hostess through the restaurant where familiar faces, famous faces, nod or wave at me. Kate looks appropriately awed, and I'm feeling like the luckiest tour guide in the world until we're brought to a very small and very tight booth with an obvious seating capacity of four people.

"I'm so sorry," the hostess says as Dad and Geoffrey shove themselves into one side of the booth, leaving Kate, Blair, and me to negotiate the other. "It's either this or the bar."

"I don't know about you," I whisper to Kate, "but I could sure use a drink."

"Damn straight," Kate says and then she slides into the booth first. I follow, then Blair, leaving me sandwiched between the past I'd like to forget and the future I hope to create.

The waitress takes our orders, and we follow Dad, Master Chef of the Blended Green Goo, who advises we stick with protein, but not too much. We both order a petite cut of steak with a side of green vegetables.

"Good choices," Dad says after the waitress leaves. "Nobody can fly when they're weighed down by a full stomach."

The comment has definitely turned Kate's mind to the competition and she looks plenty weighed down, but not with food. "Could we drive over to the Nordic Plaza after dinner?" she asks. "I'd like to see what it looks like."

My chest tightens when I think of how new and scary everything must feel to her. A glimpse, one quick glimpse, would give her something to picture as she prepares herself mentally for the next two days. Unfortunately, I know Dad's answer.

"Sorry, Kate, but they close at six."

Wave after wave of anxiety comes off her, but there's isn't one damn thing I can do except hold her hand beneath the table, and it's helping. I can feel her breath slowing, her calm vibes returning, but then Dad decides talk medicine is what Kate needs and it really pisses me off. The way parents believe talking is the solution for everything. Shouldn't that stupidity alone be grounds for firing them from their masters of the universe roles?

"But we'll head over first thing tomorrow morning for your trial round where you'll get a feel for the jump. It's a K90, same as back home with the same K Point and same landing zone. Then there's round one of jumping."

Kate asks, "And Sunday?"

Dad nods. "Same schedule. Another trial jump and round two of jumping. That's all there is to it. Of course, you'll be up against the best competitors in the sport and there will be judges and sponsors and reporters and an audience, but other than that, it's the same thing you've done hundreds—" He catches himself. "I mean, dozens of times before. All you have to do is block out everyone and everything and fly."

"That's all, huh?" Kate says. "Sounds easy."

"Exactly!" Dad says, and I cringe. He's not fluent in the language of Kate sarcasm like I am. "Just imagine you're back at Gravity Lab and you'll be fine."

Dad's mouth desperately needs something to do other than talk. Where is that damn waitress?

"I'm starved." I reach for the bread basket on the table and hold it out to Dad.

"Thanks," he says. One mission accomplished.

I take a slice because I have to, since I declared I was starving and everything. Not because I want to. It's some multigrain crap that looks like it'll leave bits of birdseed in my teeth. Gross. I take a bite and immediately wish spitting food out in public was considered a perfectly reasonable response to birdseed bread.

Kate looks around the restaurant and I watch as she recognizes faces. The smile I understand. Even the hint of intimidation. But that puzzled look? What's that about?

Kate turns to Dad. "I don't get it, Coach. It seems like everyone in the U.S. into ski jumping lives in Utah. Why did you build Gravity Lab in Minnesota?"

The corners of Dad's eyes tighten. Slightly. Most people wouldn't notice it, but I do.

Even though it's a question I've thrown at Dad a million times over the years, I know his answer is the last thing he wants to talk about right now. My mind scrambles for a way to change the subject when Blair, fucking Blair, reminds everyone she's not most people. She's my ex, which means she was practically family, which means she knows all our stories.

Blair leans over me, the better to talk at Kate, and her long hair falls over my arm, tickling my skin. "Coach wanted to build Gravity Lab here, but Ellie's mom was finishing her master's degree in instrumental performance at McNally Smith in Minneapolis and she didn't want to transfer schools, right Coach?"

Dad nods and Blair keeps talking, telling Kate stories she should have heard from me.

"So Coach moved to Minnesota and built Gravity Lab in Lutsen to be closer to her. Then, of course, they fell in love and got married and Mrs. E moved to Lutsen even though she wouldn't be able to pursue her career as a violinist as easily. I always thought that was so romantic, giving up your dream for the person you love, but now I suppose it's just sad. Because, you know—"

Jesus, it's like watching an unstoppable train wreck.

"Because...?" Kate's hand clamps down on mine.

Dad closes his eyes. I wish I could block it all out so easily, but Blair, fucking Blair, won't stop talking.

"Because last year Mrs. E auditioned for the Boston Philharmonic without telling Coach and when she was accepted, she up and left. Isn't that the saddest story you've ever heard?"

"One of them," Kate says, which is when I lose the circulation in my fingers.

Needless to say, Kate is not interested in watching the sunset over the Wasatch Mountains after dinner, though she does want to walk back to the hotel, alone, and evidently in the wrong direction.

"Kate!" I call out to her as she charts a course for Salt Lake City. "The hotel's the other way."

She turns around and her eyes are the color of gray-blue clouds, barely holding in the downpour. "Why, Ellie? I don't get it. I told you about him."

The *him* reference I understand: Kate's gambling addict dad who is too stupid to know his winning lottery ticket has been home with his daughter all along. Asshole. I even understand why I didn't tell her about Mom leaving, though thinking the answer is bad enough. I could never tell Kate that rebound rules don't require reciprocal sharing.

She clenches her fists, looking more like she's trying to hold in hurt rather than inflict it on me, though I'd gladly take the punch if it made her feel better.

"Nothing?" she asks. "You have nothing to say to me?"

I have so much to say to her, but a bunch of useless words tumble around in my head.

"Whatever," she mutters and all I do is stand there and watch her walk away.

I look up, like some divine being is going to skywrite advice for me, but the light is fading fast. Just like my relationship with Kate. I'm about to write off the whole divine being dispensing relationship advice in the sky theory when the setting sun touches the highest peak of Wasatch and everything is revealed. So many trails. So many paths. One loops uselessly and leads nowhere but down.

The rebound trail, my heart names it.

I look at the others, all heading toward the summit. Steep? Sure. Risky? Undoubtedly. Worth it? Absolutely.

"Wait!" I shout at Kate who is walking as fast as she can to get away from me. We're in the middle of the Redstone area, but I don't give a damn who hears me as long as she does. "I love you!"

She slows to a stop and turns to stare at me. "What did you say?" Kate searches my face like she's looking for some landmark she recognizes.

But she's not the one who has been lost.

"I said, I love you. I'm a total stupid idiot for not telling you sooner, but I do. I mean, I am." Jesus, is there anything my mouth can't screw up? I take a deep breath. "What I'm trying to say is, I'm in love with you, Kate."

Her face softens, but then the softness deepens into pain and I know she's still wondering why I didn't tell her about Mom.

I blurt out a truth I didn't know until that moment. "I told you she was coming home because that's what I needed to believe."

"I understand that," Kate says softly.

"You do?" I ask and the tears that well up in my eyes surprise even me.

"Unfortunately, yeah."

"So we're—?"

I don't know who takes the first step toward whom, probably me, but then Kate's in my arms again and I don't have to finish my question to know the answer.

"It's about time, El," Kate whispers. "No way was I going to say it first."

I shut her up with a kiss as the sun slips behind the mountain. We've finally found our way to the summit together and there's no way I'm letting Kate miss the view.

CHAPTER NINETEEN

There's a light breeze and crisp blue skies beckoning the jumpers at the Nordic Plaza on Saturday, and by noon we've completed all the routine tasks. We've changed into our jumpsuits, which makes Kate look even sexier, though I wouldn't have thought that possible. We've gone through the official training session, taken our trials, and been reunited with friends.

"It's like a friggin' United Nations," Kate whispers to me, and I laugh because she's right. But I've become so used to it I hardly notice the greetings in German, Norwegian, Swedish, Japanese, Slovenian, Italian, Finnish, French, and, of course, *Good to see you*, in English, though sometimes the Canadians say, *Good to see you, eh.*

Kate notices everything except, thankfully, the questioning glances shot at me when she's not looking. I answer, *Yeah, she belongs here*, in the universal language of a nod. I'm not sure if my message reaches everyone, but it will as soon as Kate racks up the points on the first jump of round one. Bibs are assigned and I'm given number three, meaning I'll be the third to jump. Kate gets number eight, which sucks. She needs to fly. The sooner, the better.

By twelve thirty, half an hour before round one, the Nordic Plaza has filled with fans waving massive cardboard signs above their heads that read things like *Here's to Hendrickson!* or *Take it, Takanashi!* A sports reporter who covers ski jumping has also arrived and is making his rounds.

The competition hasn't even begun and already I'm sweating at the thought of being interviewed on television.

"Eleanor Engebretsen!" The reporter shoves a microphone in my face, but all I can see is his fake smile and his whiter than white teeth. This is the one part of the sport I hate, the endless need to hawk the Eleanor Engebretsen brand. Isn't it enough that I jump football fields at sixty miles per hour? I have to be charming, too?

Kate, the traitor, blends into the masses. Dad pulls himself away from a conversation with another coach and walks over to take up his position behind Mr. Fake Smile and next to the cameraman. "How are you feeling about your chances today?"

"Good. Yeah, good," I answer and Dad cringes. "Really good," I add.

"Score well this weekend and you're almost guaranteed a spot on the national team. Good timing with the 2018 Olympics coming up. Tell me, Eleanor, what are your goals for today?"

"To kick some serious ass," I say, and behind Mr. Fake Smile, Dad appears to be having an aneurism. "And to jump well, too, of course."

The reporter nods and waves his hand around the Nordic Plaza where every printable surface is advertising Visa, USANA, Viessmann, OMV, Nike, and a bunch of other logos for corporate sponsors. "And what's the latest news on an endorsement deal for you?"

I shoot a questioning glance at Dad who mouths one word to me. *Lie.*

That I can do. In fact, it should be a cinch.

"We're considering several offers, but I haven't made a decision yet," I answer and Dad nods approvingly.

Mr. Fake Smile leans toward me. "Can you tell me who's in the running?"

I glance at the chairlift where Kate is waiting alone for me. Apparently everyone else has already headed up to the Nordic jump station, which means I'm wasting precious preparation time.

"Not yet." I add an edge to my voice that says I'm done with this interview. "But you'll be the first to know."

Mr. Fake Smile turns to flash his whiter than white teeth at the camera. "That was Eleanor Engebretsen, one of the most promising jumpers on the scene today…"

In the history of interviews I've given, this one isn't even near the bottom, but Dad shrugs and heads to the coach's stand.

Fuck it.

"How'd it go?" Kate asks when I join her on the chairlift platform.

"Who cares?" I answer. "It's time to kick ass, not kiss ass."

"You got that right," she says as we feel the familiar bump against the back of our knees and sit down.

We're halfway up to the jump when it dawns on us. Or maybe it dawns on me and Kate's known it all along. I don't know. We reach the top and step away from the chairlift. She to the right and I to the left. There's distance between us. Not much, but it still feels beyond weird and we stare at each other. The whole *off the hill we're friends, but on the hill we're competitors* speech doesn't seem to apply when it begins with *off the hill we're lovers.*

Kate walks over to me and brushes a strand of hair from my face. "May the best woman win," she says as she turns and walks across the metal grate that leads to the Nordic jump station. As usual, she's a few steps ahead of me.

❖

Anyone looking to feel like a badass jumper for a weekend will be sorely disappointed if they stumble into the Nordic jump station where they will not sit by a crackling fireplace or admire antique skis mounted on the wall or tip back an eight dollar shot of vodka. They will find themselves in a large concrete building attached to the K90 jump where the few comforts are a warming room with windows that overlook the jump, a soda machine, and a few benches. Oh, and there's a nice open space to stretch or pace or zen out, whatever it takes to get in the headspace where crazy impossible becomes perfectly sane and even exciting.

Kate and I enter the warming room filled with six or seven jumpers...and Blair.

"Oh my God!" Blair squeals. "I thought I was going to faint when I sat on the start bar for the trial! That jump is totally insane!" Her voice bounces off hard concrete walls and stone faces. A quick glance around the room tells me she's about ten seconds from being thrown down the jump headfirst.

Blair spots me, stands, and talks as she charges toward me. "Finally! Ellie, your dad totally lied. This is so not like the jump at Gravity Lab."

Fuck. She's Geoffrey-with-a-*G*'s responsibility now, but he's on the large hill, waiting to compete against the other male jumpers. Jerk. Totally useless jerk.

I sigh and look at Kate.

She nods. "It's cool. Talk her down. Duct-tape her mouth. Do whatever it takes." Kate moves away and sits on a bench where she watches with an amused look as Blair corners me next to the soda machine.

"Blair, quit freaking out," I tell her. "It's the same height. Same K Point. Same outrun."

"I am not freaking out," Blair lies. "And it's not the same. I don't care about height and crap like that. It is *not* the same!" Her eyes are wide and she's clenching and unclenching her hands. Shit. I've seen plenty of jumpers react to their first competition like this. It's the pressure to win and not simply jump for fun. It never ends well for jumpers who force themselves into competition before they're ready.

The name for the first jumper is called, which means I don't have time to dance around Blair's feelings.

"You know you don't have to do this, right?" I ask, and I can practically measure how fast the question sinks in by how long it takes her to stop twitching and shaking.

"Are you telling me to quit?" She stares at me.

"I'm telling you to ask yourself why you're here."

"I, ah…" Blair looks confused. "I mean, I thought…"

"Not good enough." My voice slices through her babbling, but time is running out. For both of us. "You have to know, deep down, that you want this more than anything, or you shouldn't be here."

That's when her bottom lip starts to tremble.

The announcer's voice blasts through the overhead speaker. "That was a beautiful first jump of the day earning fifty-eight points for distance and fifty points for style. We're off to a good start!"

My brain does a quick calculation. One hundred and eight points. Tough, but beatable.

"Get out of here, Blair. Grab your skis and take the chairlift back down. Tell an official you're withdrawing from the competition. Got it?"

Her eyes flash defiantly. Gone is the trembling lip. "I get that you don't think I can handle it. I also get you don't want me in any part of your life now."

True, on both counts, but that isn't the point. "Blair, what I don't want is to see you lying at the bottom of that jump in pieces." I even feel a little warm and fuzzy toward her because I don't want her hurt. It's possible I never did.

"You do still care." She reaches up like she's going to hug me.

Girl's lost her damn mind.

I sidestep her. "Go. Get out of here. Get your hair done. Get a mani-pedi. Get the volume pack of condoms, size small, for your boyfriend. Just don't get on that jump."

She looks hurt. Also a little pissed. Fine by me though, because for once, Blair Caldwell does as she's told and ditches the warming room. I glance out the window and see the second jumper moving onto the start bar, which means I'm on deck. Not much time left, but I know exactly how to spend it.

"How are you doing?" I sit beside Kate.

"Fine." She smiles. "That was a good thing you did for Blair."

I shake my head. "I'm asking about you. How are you doing?"

Kate takes a deep breath and exhales. "I am okay." And it's there in her eyes, the look I've seen in every great jumper's eyes. The certainty they were born to do this crazy thing. The knowledge they are right where they belong.

I lean over and kiss her cheek. "Do one thing for me?"

"Sure," she says. "What?"

"Fly. Like you've never flown before."

She nods and her eyes look beyond me, like she's imagining herself sitting on that start bar. Good. She's entering her zone and she doesn't need me to distract her.

"See you at the bottom?" I stand up. It's time.

"Save a place for me," she says, and I'm about to say *of course*, when she adds, "preferably in the top three."

I walk onto the open platform, still laughing and loving Kate, when a gust of cold air slaps me into reality.

"You next?" a friend I've known for years asks me with a thick Slovenian accent.

I point at the number three on my bib. "Yep."

"Have one, El," she says to me.

Have one. It's what we say to each other moments before a jump. Have a great flight, the time of your life, a safe landing so you can fly again soon. *Have one.*

"Thanks," I say. "You, too."

The announcer's voice blasts the second jumper's score. Sixty-two points for distance. Fifty-two points for style. I delete the number one hundred and eight and record one hundred fourteen in my mind.

Tough, but still beatable.

Minutes, that's all I've got. I pace and breathe and pace and breathe until the clanging thoughts, one by one, float away.

Blair? Mom? They've chosen their lives.

And Kate?

Did she choose this life with me?

Of course she did. I walk down three steps, sit on the start bar, and put on my skis.

A lie stops being a lie when it becomes the truth.

I bend over and secure the bindings.

It's real. Now.

I scoot over until I'm centered.

It doesn't matter how it began.

To my right, near the takeoff, are the grandstand for coaches and the station for judges. Far below me is the sea of people, tiny little people, their eyes fixed on me. Expecting things of me.

But there's only one person whose opinion matters to me now. I look over at the warming room, knowing she'll be there. My girl, framed in the window, smiling at me.

I pull my goggles over my eyes, slip on my gloves, grip the start bar, and begin rocking. Back and forth, back and forth.

A wall of mountains in front of me.

A mountain of lies behind me.

Finally, it comes. The moment when it's easier to let go than to hold on, and I push off. Speed down the inrun. Hit the takeoff. Spring forward.

And begin my dance with gravity.

The earth tugs at me, and I would fall, fast and hard, if it weren't for the fact that I'm flying *on* air, not simply *through* it. I move my skis into a V formation and turn my hands, extended behind me and parallel with my body, palms up. Most jumpers keep their fingers touching, but not me. I fan mine out and hold on to the cushion of air between me and the hard ground for as long as possible.

This is my time. My turn. It's right in front of me. The K Point. The rushing ground. My future. I move my legs, one in front of the other. Shift my balance and touch down, textbook Telemark style. In the distance, from the coaches' stand, I hear Dad screaming, "That's my girl!"

I ski into the outrun toward people I don't even know, held back by the barrier, but cheering for me. It's weird. And pretty wonderful.

I turn and look at the judges' station. Like they're going to hold up cards with the numbers 1–20 written on them or something. It doesn't work that way, but I can't look away.

Time stops. My heart skips a beat. God's finger hits the pause button on my life.

And then the announcer shouts, "Eleanor Engebretsen has taken the lead with a distance score of sixty-four and a style score of fifty-six!"

One hundred and twenty calculates itself in my mind.

I bend over and grab my sides. Ten years of my life. Countless jumps, hours in the gym, green goo for breakfast—all for this moment.

I stand, raise my arm above my head, and the Nordic Plaza explodes with the sound of cheering voices.

Then the moment is over and my thoughts return to the girl wearing bib number eight, alone in a warming room full of strangers and dreaming of the chance to change her life.

Number four jumps.

Number five.

Number six.

Number seven.

No, they're not numbers to me. They're people, friends, fellow jumpers, but right now there's only one name on my mind.

Kate Moreau.

I can see her sitting on the start bar, barely, but I can't miss her when she speeds down the inrun and leaps into the air.

It's possible I may have an aneurism.

Then she transitions into a gorgeous flight formation. Weak ankles, Dad? I don't think so. There's nothing weak about Kate.

She flies. Damn, does she fly and it's a beautiful thing to see. She drops, of course, bit by bit, but not before she blows past the

K Point. She touches down. Not precisely a Telemark landing, but she'll nail that, too, and soon.

Kate skis into the outrun and joins me by the gates. High-fiving is normal. Hugging? Not so much, but neither of us cares.

Kate is flushed, radiant, nervous as hell.

"You killed it," I tell her, truthfully.

The wait for her score stretches into forever.

"What's taking so long?" She shifts her weight and kicks her skis against the ground.

"It takes a while, you know," I tell her. "Adding up a score that high."

She smiles. Quiets her body and her feet.

Finally, the announcer breaks the tension. "Katherine Moreau, jumper number eight, has earned sixty-eight for distance and forty-five for style points!"

The calculator in my mind gets to work. One hundred thirteen. Holy shit.

The crowd goes wild. Mr. Fake Smile's voice comes from behind and startles me. "Congrats on your great first jump. Mind if I ask a question?"

I turn to answer him, but his microphone is pointing directly at Kate.

"Me?" She stares at Mr. Fake Smile. "You want to interview me?"

"Absolutely! If that's okay with you, Katherine."

Kate nods. "Yeah, sure. But call me Kate, okay?"

The reporter laughs. "Kate, it is. First question is one everyone here wants to know." He waves toward the crowd in the Nordic Plaza. "Who is Kate Moreau and where did she come from?"

Kate stares at a clump of snow on her skis for a second before she lifts her head and looks directly at Mr. Fake Smile.

"I, ah, I'm originally from Tahoe, but that's boring. Are you sure you want to interview me?"

Two seconds into her first interview and she's genuine. Vulnerable. Charmingly awkward. I should be taking notes.

"Honey," Mr. Fake Smile says, "everyone's going to want to interview you before the day is over, but I want to be the first to get the scoop on Kate Moreau, formerly from boring Tahoe and now in the top three at the International Continental Cup. Why don't you tell me how you got here."

I'm half expecting Kate to answer *on a plane*, but her face settles into her serious look. She takes a few seconds and I can practically hear Dad shouting, *No dead air!* But like everything else with Kate, her answer is worth the wait.

"I guess I'm here because I'm lucky." Kate pauses, drawing the reporter in without even trying. She's a natural at more than jumping. "I grew up jumping off beds, snowbanks, anything I could find, the way lots of kids do, and nobody thought I was particularly talented. Annoying, maybe, but definitely not talented." She gives a made-for-ratings smile. "Then I moved to Minnesota this year where I met Ellie and Coach Engebretsen. They saw something in me and wanted to train me. The truth is, I'm here because they believed in me."

Mr. Fake Smile needs a new name. "Amazing, Kate. You. Your talent. Your story." Mr. Sappy Smile turns to the camera. "That was Kate Moreau, a complete unknown from Minnesota who trails her fellow teammate and mentor, Eleanor Engebretsen, by a mere seven points. It's an exciting day of ski jumping at the Utah Olympic Park, and the question on everybody's mind is whether Kate Moreau can keep her position after her second jump. We'll know soon enough, but one thing is certain. Kate Moreau is a wildcard worth watching."

Kate's second jump answers Mr. Sappy Smile's question. With a combined score of 225.3, she closed the gap between us by three points. Bottom line, she kicked my ass in distance, but I scored more points in form. Of course, we're fighting it out for second since a jumper from Japan snagged first with a combined score of 234.2, but it's all good. Today Kate and I claimed ground. Tomorrow we'll defend it.

But tonight? Tonight we celebrate.

My spot on the National team and endorsement money is practically guaranteed and that's freaking awesome. But what's even better is the future I see for Kate. This could be her life. Better yet, this could be our life together.

"Meet me in my room?" I ask Kate as we walk into the lobby of the Newpark Resort and ride an empty elevator to our floor.

"Sure, but after I soak in a tub. I hurt in places I didn't know existed." Kate groans. "Give me an hour?"

My head gets it. Even my ass does. It's feeling the effects of the day, too. But other parts of me are convinced an hour is way too long to wait for Kate's hands to be on me, and those parts, apparently, are in charge.

"Thirty minutes," I tell her. "Forty-five tops. Any longer and I'll hop in that tub with you and start the celebration there."

The elevator stops and I walk Kate to her room.

"This has been the best day of my life, El," Kate says. "I don't know how to thank you."

I find a way by giving her lips something else to do.

Kate breaks off our kiss, muttering about muscles and tubs and aching. The last word is the only one that registers with me. Aching, I understand.

"Thirty minutes," I tell her. "And then I'm coming in after you."

Once in my room, I open my suitcase, pull out the ridiculous outfit I bought to wear for Kate, and lay it on the bed. *Lingerie*, the saleslady called it, and I wanted to barf all over the underwear display. But I bought the silk camisole, sheer in all the right places with a built in bra—if two strips of fabric can be called a bra. I bought the matching pair of thong underwear, too, though I wish someone would've told me thongs are dental floss for butt cheeks. I'm going to look ridiculous. I'm going to feel even more ridiculous, but Kate's going to laugh her ass off when she sees me in the getup, and I can't think of a better way to begin our celebration than with the sound of her laugh.

I unzip my jeans and let them fall on the floor. My shirt and underwear and socks follow, and then I'm holding the thong in my hands and studying it like it's a goddamn geometry problem to solve. Eventually I figure it out, pull it on, and rid my asshole of tartar buildup. The camisole top is trickier than I remembered in the changing room. How does anyone shove boobs into strips of fabric no bigger than Band-Aids and keep everything in place? There are a few wardrobe malfunctions, but ultimately I find myself standing in the middle of my room, looking at my reflection in the mirror.

It's…it's…pretty damn horrifying. I grab the extra blanket off the foot of the bed and wrap it around me until the mirror and I are no longer enemies. Outside the sky is changing colors again so I pull the chair in front of the window and watch the Wasatch Mountains flair to life with the setting sun. This time, there's no question about my path. Only sweet thoughts about the sunsets and summits Kate and I will share together.

A sharp rap of knuckles on my room door startles me. It hasn't been half an hour. I smile. Kate's as impatient as I am though why she's not using the connecting door is a mystery. I drop the blanket, walk across the room, and open the door.

"Kate, I thought you were—"

Shock shuts down my vocal cords when Blair, her hair tied in a casual knot on top of her head, dressed in pink from her thermal top to her flannel pants to her fuzzy slippers, stands in front of me.

"I want to talk to you," she says and then she gets an eyeful of me in my lingerie and I don't know what's worse, the amused look on her face or the fact that she's looking past me into an obviously empty room. "Unless I'm interrupting something?"

"N-no," I stammer because I have no idea how to explain why I'm standing, half naked, in my room by myself.

"Good." She waltzes in and sits on my bed. "Then we can talk." Behind me the door clicks shut. The walls of the room press in. The stupid outfit I'm wearing shrinks, something I would not have believed possible.

I scan the floor and spot the blanket lying at the foot of the bed. "Do you mind?" I point and she looks down, but leaves it right where it is.

"Not at all."

Hmm, stand there, giving Blair a free front-row seat at a peep show, or jiggle and bounce my way past her to grab the blanket and reclaim some dignity?

Not a hard choice to make.

I scoop up the blanket from the floor and wrap it around my body like it's a towel and I'm fresh from the shower. "What's left to talk about, Blair?"

"You. Me," she says. "What happened with us."

Is she for real? "There is absolutely nothing you have to say that would interest me, but I would love to hear the sound of the door closing behind you."

She doesn't blink. Doesn't move. "That's twice you've tried to kick me out of a room today except this time it's not going to work. There's stuff you don't know that you need to hear, and I'm not leaving until you do."

Fuck. It's not like I can physically throw her out. I shuffle across the room, dragging the blanket behind me like some demented wedding train, and plop my ass in the chair by the window. Once I'm completely tucked and covered, I swivel to face her. "Fine. You've got about five minutes. Talk fast."

She shakes her head. "You know, you were nicer before you started dating Kate," she says.

"And you were more faithful before you started fucking Geoffrey," I lash back.

The comment hangs in the air between us for a few seconds, and then Blair breaks eye contact. "I deserve that."

"I thought you were here to tell me something I didn't know." It rises in me, the anger I thought had disappeared along with my feelings for her.

"I am." Blair looks at me again and I swear her eyes are shiny. "You think I left you for Geoffrey because I didn't love you, but you're wrong."

That's when my Blair Bullshit-o-meter blows. "How about we get the facts right? You didn't *leave* me. You sent me a text." When did I spring out of the chair? When did the blanket slip from my shoulders? I don't know and I don't care. I am the jar and Blair, stupid fucking Blair, is Pandora and she deserves whatever flies out of me. "That's how I found out you were fucking Geoffrey. That's how I found out we were over. Through a goddamn text that wasn't even meant for me. And all along I thought you were different. That you weren't like…that you could never be like…"

Blair stands and faces me. "Your mom," she says. "You believed I would never leave you like she did. With no warning. Without even saying good-bye."

I'm shaking, but not from cold.

She tries to pull me into her arms, but I turn away because the tears are threatening to come and she cannot see me crying. God, she cannot.

"El, that's what I'm here to tell you and what you don't know. I am sorry. So sorry. You deserved better from both of us. I can't apologize for her, El, but I can for me."

The tears have retreated. I risk a glance at her and damned if she doesn't look like Blair again. My Blair. But of course she isn't. She's Geoffrey-with-a-*G*'s Blair. Or is she? I don't know anything. Not anymore.

"I did love you," she says. "So much. I want you to know that. But there wasn't any room for me in your life. There was only jumping, jumping, jumping, all the while reaching for the gold and never for me."

Her words feel so true.

And so false.

"I reached for you plenty!"

She shakes her head. "My body, El. You reached for my body. Never for me."

I suddenly feel more naked than ever, stripped of even my anger. I look at Blair and see the girl I should have seen all along. Not mine. Not Geoffrey's. Not the star in some bitch project.

She's Blair.

The girl in stupid fuzzy pink slippers with two-toned hair tumbling over her face.

"Anyway, that's what I came to say. I'll go now," she says, but she doesn't.

"I'm sorry, too, Blair." I say words I never thought I'd say, much less mean. "Are you happy?"

"With Geoffrey?" she shrugs. "I'm not unhappy."

I remember how I felt when Kate told me we were not *not* okay. I want more than that for Blair.

"What about you?" she asks me. "Are you happy, El?"

"I am, Blair. More than I ever thought possible."

"I'm glad." She pulls me into her arms and whispers in my ear, "And all this time I thought losing me didn't hurt you at all. That's why you were able to move on so fast and begin dating Kate." Her voice is loud enough to block out the creaking of a door, but soft enough for me to tell her the truth.

"Losing you almost killed me," I say. "I started dating Kate to try to forget you. It was just a rebound thing." I am about to add *at first, but not anymore* when a voice, not mine and not Blair's, interrupts and I don't get the chance.

"Just a rebound thing?"

Blair pulls away, fast and all at once, but still too slow. I turn toward the voice and see Kate's face, flooded with pain.

"I'm just a rebound to you," she says again, though this time it's a statement, not a question.

PART IV: THE K POINT

I was maybe eight, when I finally asked Dad why the steepest point on the hill was called the K Point. By then I'd been jumping long enough to know it was where I was supposed to land, if not fly past. Long enough to hear other jumpers call it the construction point or the calculation point sometimes. And though I didn't know how to spell those words, I knew neither of them began with a *K*.

Construction point made no sense. That sounded like something a person built. Like a tree fort or a candy store or a Lego castle. But I was eight. I still believed God had made the earth and the sky, and it seemed wrong for people to take credit for his hill.

Calculation point made even less sense. My calculator helped me in my math classroom, not on a ski jump. That word buzzed in my head and couldn't attach to anything with meaning until Dad entered me in my first competition and I learned I was not the only girl my age who flew like a bird. There were lots of us, and we were part of the same flock, though we were not all treated the same. Some girls went home after the competitions with medals or ribbons and some went home with nothing, all because a judge added up some numbers. It didn't make sense. Didn't the judges know the real prize was the feeling of flying, and every girl had won? I couldn't puzzle it out until the day I lay in the grass in the shadow of a naked tree, breathing in the scent of dusty leaves, and watching geese fly south for the winter. Like me, they flew in a V formation. And like my flock, one goose had been singled out to lead while the others followed. The geese seemed okay with that arrangement so I tried to be, too. It got easier once I started winning.

After I ran out of thumbtacks from hanging ribbons on my bedroom wall, I still didn't know what the *K* in K Point stood for, so one day I asked Dad.

"It comes from the German word *kritical*," he said and wrote it down for me. He said it had the same meaning as the English word critical, but it didn't sound at all the same when he said it in German. His *k*'s and *t*'s were harsher. His *i*'s were clipped short and sharp. The word sent chills through my body then, and it still does. Nothing else has ever made me understand more clearly what's at stake when I cross a line.

Whether it's a bright red line painted in the snow at the steepest point of a hill and I'm supposed to cross it. Or it's a line, drawn by an auburn-haired girl at the deepest point of her pain, that she trusts me not to cross.

It doesn't get more *kritical* than that.

CHAPTER TWENTY

I sit on the bed in my room, trying to think of what I can say to Kate. But that's the thing about lies. You tell yarn after yarn after yarn, and right when you find the thread your heart wants to follow, your whole damn life becomes one god-awful, tangled mess.

Shit.

I stand and open the connecting door that leads to Kate's room. I shouldn't be surprised or hurt that her door is closed and locked, but I am.

"Kate? Please let me in," I say, but the door remains shut. I never meant to use Kate. I only wanted to stop feeling the pain, and one day there was no pain, only love. For Kate. She'll understand that, won't she? Who am I kidding? Of course she won't. She was never given the script for The Blair Bitch Project. She thought this was real, all along, because I told her it was.

Fuck, I *told* her it was.

How could I have done that?

I clench my fists. This wasn't all my fault. This wasn't even mainly my fault. It was Blair's. She hurt me in the first place. And Jack's. Yeah. Fucking Jack! She was the one who told me to get over Blair by throwing myself into a relationship, any relationship. Jack never said one word about what I should do when the feelings became real, so this is her fault, too. Big time.

"Kate, please let me explain." I don't quite knock, but I don't pound on the door either.

Still nothing but silence.

"Kate! Let me in!" I pound on her door, lost in a world where the door between Kate and me is sealed. But that thought threatens to send me spinning completely out of control, and I've trained my whole life not to let that happen.

I walk away from the door.

I sit on the bed and stare at the door.

I go into the bathroom and pee, come out to sit on the bed and stare at the door. Heat surges through me. If science fiction were real, I'd have laser eyes that could burn that fucking door down.

❖

I wake up on Sunday morning in that ridiculous outfit, rolled in the blanket like a burrito. Sometime during the night sleep overtook me, and a legion of fluttering monarchs took up residence in my stomach. Not because I'm facing the second day of the International Continental Cup competition, but because I'm going to have to face Kate.

The clock reads eight a.m., which means the second round of trials starts in less than two hours. Time to get my head in the game. I schlep myself out of bed and sit on the floor and try to summon an image of me flying past the K Point and nailing a perfect Telemark landing, but the screen in my mind is playing a different movie. One where Kate walks into my room and overhears words, *my* words, confiding a truth to Blair I hoped Kate would never learn.

I used her to get over Blair.

Kate didn't get to hear the rest of that sentence, though now I'm not sure it would have mattered that The Blair Bitch Project was a huge success, that I am completely over Blair and completely in love with Kate. No, pretty sure she heard the part that mattered most to her and I don't have the first clue how, or even if, I can make this right between us.

I take a quick shower and head downstairs for a complimentary breakfast of deep-fried or sugar-coated carbs. Dad, Geoffrey, and Blair are sitting around a table, drinking glasses of the protein shake Dad brings to competitions. It tastes marginally better than his blended concoction back home. I sit at the empty fourth chair where Kate should be but isn't.

To my right is Blair and there's *no way* I can look at her. She saw enough of me last night. To my left is Dad and he's hauling something from behind his chair, something I absolutely do not want to see, so I turn and beam rays of sunshine at Geoffrey-with-a-*G*. It's a fucked-up world. That's for sure.

Dad guides the suitcase with wheels around his chair and parks it in front of me. "She kept the jumpsuit, helmet, goggles, and gloves on the condition I let her pay them off in installments." He shakes his head. "Said that was all she wanted from any Engebretsen."

Message received. Ouch.

After our liquid breakfast, I unzip the suitcase and pull out the coat I gave to Kate. I slip my arms in it and it almost feels like she's hugging me. Until I put my hands in the pockets and pull out a note. At first I think it's the one I wrote for her, the one telling Cassandra White to fuck off because she didn't need her coat anymore.

Yeah, same message, but it's not for Cassandra White.

Still, I can smell her shampoo on the collar and I can't make myself take the damn coat off.

The four of us pile into the van. I don't know how Kate is getting to the Nordic Plaza, but from the items she decided to keep, I know she'll be there.

❖

Dad pulls me aside after we park at Utah Olympic Park. His face is stern, but not cold. I can't tell whose eyes I'm looking into, my dad's or my coach's. "Give her space," he says. "You both have too much riding on today's competition to be distracted with a big emotional scene."

Ah, that clarifies things.

"Not to be bitchy," I say, though I'm sure that's precisely what I'm being, "but I could use my dad's advice. Not my coach's."

He runs a hand through his white-blond hair and turns his eyes toward the mountains. I'm shitty with directions, but I'd bet he's facing northeast.

"Fine," he says. "From what I heard this morning, it's pretty clear you inherited more than athletic ability from me. You can be the world's biggest prick, too."

I can hardly believe what I'm hearing. I sure as hell don't know how to feel about it.

"Know what, Eleanor?"

"What?"

"The best people in life don't want to hang around pricks."

"But it's not like that, Dad." I glance around the Nordic Plaza and spot Kate in line for the chairlift, holding my mother's skis and wearing a jumpsuit she's buying in installments. "This is a big misunderstanding. I have to make her see that."

He shakes his head. "And I have to make you see today isn't about fixing things with Kate. You want to do right by her? Wonderful. Leave her alone. Let her have the real chance she deserves."

Shit. What am I supposed to say when he lays it out like that?

"And tomorrow?" He's looking toward the northeast again. "You do what I should have done years ago. Work your ass off to become a reformed prick, someone she actually deserves before—"

I finish his sentence. "Kate takes up the violin?"

He looks at me with more sadness in his eyes than I've ever seen before. "Something like that."

"I'm sorry, Dad."

"Don't be," he says. "I brought it on myself."

It's possible Dad and I have broken the longest ever heart-to-heart conversation record in the entire Engebretsen family history.

He looks up the K90 hill and lifts his shoulders, stands a little taller. "Now get up to the Nordic station. The International Continental Cup isn't going to wait all day for you to get your crap together."

And we're back to normal. Or what passes for normal between Dad and me.

It's pretty damn awful how much can change in twenty-four hours. A chairlift built for two becomes a lonely ride for one. The cozy warming room of yesterday is the frigid icebox of today. All it's missing is a sign on the door that reads, *No Engebretsens allowed.*

Not that it's needed. I get the message loud and clear when I enter the room and find it half full with jumpers, and Kate, who refuses to acknowledge my presence, though she's putting off an attitude so cold, I begin to worry about frostbite.

"How's everyone doing?" I play it cool and look like I'm checking in with the whole room, but Kate knows who I'm talking to.

I'm pummeled with answers.

Good.

'Bout to puke as usual.

Can't wait. Bring it on!

But from the person who counts? Nothing.

Today we'll jump in reverse order of yesterday's placings, which means the Japanese jumper will go last with me next to last and Kate right before me. But that rule doesn't apply to the trial jump and I'd just as soon get out of here so Kate can focus on the competition and not my epic failures as a girlfriend.

I leave the warming—make that chilling—room and cross the open area where I head straight for the stairs to the jump.

"You aren't going to stretch, El?" a jumper I've known since I was ten asks me.

"Already did," I lie. Which is, apparently, what I do best.

"Cool," she says. "Have one, El!"

I don't answer. I've already had one. A horrible night, the worst time of my life, and a crash landing I won't get over anytime soon.

A headwind has blown in over the mountains during the night. Like I need something else to overcome. I squat on the edge of the start bar and put on my skis. My helmet. Secure my goggles over my eyes. My gloves. Swing around to face the inrun. None of these movements require me to think. They are stored in some memory recorded over and over hundreds, make that thousands of times before.

I scoot to the center of the start bar and look for my horizon, but yesterday's blue skies have been driven away by a gray-white haze. Gone are the mountains in front of me, the tiny people below me. I shake my shoulders to loosen my upper body and look down the jump and beside it, the platform for coaches and the station for judges. Some things never change.

The start bar is cold beneath my ass. My skis glide back and forth in their grooves. My lungs expand. Contract. In and out. In and out. Five counts in. Seven counts out. They come to me, the faces, nearly transparent now and made of mist. Mother's abandoned. Blair's discarded. Good-bye and good-bye. They float away like a snowflake caught in the wind.

Another face comes to me, one I know too well. I should. It's the face that lives in mirrors.

I don't want to look at you, I tell this face.

But, of course, I do. I examine the side turned toward the light and the side hidden in shadow. I spot the ridges and ripples on cheeks and chins and foreheads.

Not a face. A mask.

A stupid papier-mâché mask made of lie layered over lie over lie, until every part of the true face is hidden.

Oh God, Kate. I'm so sorry.

I look at the window of the warming room, knowing what I will see.

Glass. Nothing but glass.

I grip the start bar and rock, back and forth, back and forth. I can't breathe. I can't see. It's this mask. This stupid mask.

I have to fly. Grab air. Feel free.

I crouch and push off, but I can tell it's not right. I can't feel the inrun beneath my feet. I can't see the takeoff either. There's no going back. I feel the speed and the fear and the panic rising, and then the jump abandons me. I'm trying to launch off thin air and my body is pitching forward. I've gone too far this time. Too fucking far. There's no going back. My arms flail. My legs move behind me instead of in front of me. My body inverts and for a second I'm a helicopter flying through the air at sixty miles per hour and then I'm plunging toward the ground. I'm gravity's bitch, weighed down by lies I thought didn't matter.

Oh God, there's no going back.

I don't see the ground when I hit, though I feel the searing heat flare along my left side. Something, deep in my shoulder, snaps. My arm goes limp before the rest of me does and I'm somersaulting down the knoll, choking on the spray of snow until I slide, like a broken and thrown away rag doll, into the outrun.

I don't know how long I lie there, facedown in the blackness, breathing in snow that tastes like metal. And I don't know how long I stay in the black world. I do know the first voice I hear is masculine and low and calm.

"We're going to turn you now, Ms. Engebretsen," the voice says. "Please don't move."

No argument from me.

Arms, strong arms, dig under the snow beneath my body. One set at my chest. Another at my hips. Another at my legs. My body rises out of the red-spotted snow and I gasp for air. My left arm flops toward the ground and I scream. I think I scream. I must scream because red sprays the snow beneath me. Another set of hands holds my arm while my body turns and turns and turns until I am lying on my back, though not on snow. No snow is this hard and comes with straps.

"I'm going to remove your goggles now so I can see your eyes."

The world explodes in searing light.

"*K-k.*" Blood sprays into the air. Some of it drops on my cheeks. In my eyes. The blinding white turns soft red until I blink it away.

"Please, Ms. Engebretsen. Don't try to talk." The voice has a nice face. Kind eyes. Bushy eyebrows.

But he doesn't understand.

"*K-Kay.*" I can't make my mouth work. Not with my whole body trembling and twitching, triggering jolts of pain that flood my brain and shut it down.

"On three," someone says. "One, two, three."

I levitate into the air.

"K-Kate," I finally say to the sky as I float through the air.

No one answers. Not even the kind voice with the bushy eyebrows.

CHAPTER TWENTY-ONE

A complex left-sided scapula fracture with extension into the glenoid and an associated midshaft clavicle fracture—that was the official diagnosis after X-rays were taken at the emergency room at the Park City Mountain Resort Ski Clinic. The unofficial diagnosis was easier to understand, if not accept. I was pretty much screwed and would be even more once I was transported to the University Hospital in Salt Lake City, where friendly orthopedic surgeons would piece my shoulder blade together.

Had I just broken my collarbone, I would have had the option to let it heal on its own. But no, when I screw a thing up, I screw it up good, so the surgeons also had to bolt a metal plate on that. They call it open reduction and internal fixation. And yeah, I felt openly reduced. But internally fixed? Not so much.

The days I spent in the hospital are mainly a blur now that I'm home in Lutsen with my new best friend, morphine. Jack's acting all hurt about losing her BFF status, but in an arm-wrestling contest over who's hurting the most, she'd lose. Even with my arm in a sling. Besides, she's got a new sidekick, too. Alex, the hot and heavily tattooed Alex from Pandora's Box. Jack visited the evening I got home, but that was a week ago. Since then all I've gotten are texts saying things like, *El, I think I'm in love*. It sucks, being stuck at home, body and heart broken, while my best friend is too busy spending time with her girlfriend to visit, but I am happy for Jack. Shocked, but happy.

"Yo, El?" Jack's voice shoots up the staircase. "You home?"

"No, I'm riding a chairlift up Mount Kilimanjaro. Want to join me?"

Jack walks into the living room. I expected Alex to be glued to her side, but she's alone.

"Any reply yet?" she asks.

I answer by scowling out the window at Lake Superior. We're both cracking at about the same pace thanks to an early March thaw and the fact that Kate hasn't returned one of my calls or texts.

"Fuck. I'm sorry." Jack glances around the living room. "Did you get a new couch?"

"Yeah," I answer from my perma-place on the La-Z-Boy Dad bought for his La-Z-Girl. Damn thing has more flexibility than I do with footrests that extend and a back that reclines, but I love it. Even if it is a color Dad calls chocolate brown and I call shade o' shit. Not that I'd know much about shitting lately. My new best friend comes with a few wicked side effects.

Jack sits on the matching chair by the window.

"Where's Alex?" I ask.

"That's done." Jack clenches her jaw, but it's not anger I'm reading on her face. It's another emotion, one I know too well.

"I'm sorry," I tell her, meaning it.

"Don't be. I'm heading to Duluth tonight. My cousin says there's a whole new crowd of ladies at Pandora's Box and they're smoking hot."

Unfuckingbelievable.

"Hey, I bought something for you." Jack hands me a Barnes & Noble bag. "Thought it might cheer you up."

I pull out the book and read the title. "*An Abundance of Katherines* by John Green? You've got to be kidding me."

Jack leans forward. "Naw, El. It's just what you need right now. It's a great book about this guy named Colin who's totally a genius, except he falls in love with girl after girl, all of them named Katherine. Nineteen total, can you believe that? Anyway, Katherine number nineteen breaks Colin's heart so much, he takes off on this epic road trip with his buddy Hassan and winds up in a weird town where everybody works at a tampon factory."

"A what?" I can't have heard Jack right.

"A tampon factory, but that's not the point. Finally, at the end of the book, Colin—"

"Let me guess," I interrupt. "Colin realizes there's such an abundance of Katherines he's able to move on to number twenty after he has mind-blowing rebound sex with a stranger."

Jack nods her head. "Exactly! See? That's how the book should have ended, but Colin falls for a girl named Lindsey from the weird tampon factory town. You'd think a *New York Times* best seller like JG would have caught that mistake."

"Oh, Jack." I don't even know where to begin. "Has it ever occurred to you that the mistake is thinking one girl can replace another?"

Jack pulls back in her chair and stares out the window. "You know what? You're both nuts. You and John Green." She gets up and leaves in a huff. Jack probably thinks I'm blaming her for losing Kate because The Blair Bitch Project bombed, but I'm not.

Anymore.

It took the side of a mountain to knock sense into me, but at least now I know. I'm at fault. Me. Not Jack. Not Blair. Not Mom. *Me.* I lost Kate because I once thought the way Jack still does, and I'm sad. For me. For Kate. For Jack. For every girl who happens to be at Pandora's Box tonight.

I look at the cover of the book and shake my head.

There may be an abundance of Katherines, but there's only one Kate. At least for me.

I grab the remote control and turn on the television and pull up the footage of the International Continental Cup Dad set the TiVo to record before we flew to Utah. At the time he thought he'd be capturing my finest hour. Now? It's…I don't know. High definition pain on a forty-eight inch flat screen?

It's also the only thing I have left of Kate.

I've watched the footage so many times I've memorized every word of her first interview when she was still my Kate, sweet and surprised anyone even knew her name. I've also memorized every word of her other interview after she won second place and she was still sweet, less surprised, and no longer mine.

Most nights I fall asleep in the living room on the new couch watching the video footage. Sitting up hurts a hell of a lot less than lying down. So does listening to Kate's voice, rather than her silence. I wake up every morning in my bed though. I assume Dad waits until I'm out, thanks to the sound of Kate's voice and the highest dose of painkillers I'm allowed, and carries me into my room. Some nights I dream Dad talks to me while I'm sleeping. They don't feel like any dreams I've had before, but they must be because he tells me things Dad would never say. Like he loves me and he's so sorry I'm in pain and he'd take it all from me if he could. One night I even dream Dad is sitting on one of the dining room chairs next to my bed, talking to Mom on his cell.

She's fine, Irina. Getting stronger every day, I promise…A violin concerto next week? Of course, Eleanor will understand.

I wake up the next morning, convinced my dream was real, but the dining room chair has vanished from my room as completely as my mother has vanished from my life.

Doc's got me on some trippy drugs, that's for sure.

"Eleanor, are you hungry?" Dad pokes his head out of the kitchen about an hour after Jack has left. Scents I haven't smelled since Mom left float toward me. Meat cooking. Bread baking. My stomach growls.

"Not really." I pause the video on Kate's face. "But thanks."

Dad mutters something I don't catch, and I see the door to the kitchen close out of the corner of my eye. I pick up my phone and check my messages.

Nothing.

Pathetic, I know. Even worse, I type, *I miss you, I'm so proud of you, and I'm so sorry*, and hit send. Which brings the one-way message count to forty-three. I'll qualify as a stalker soon.

I fast-forward the video to Kate's last jump, the one where she nailed her Telemark landing and secured second place. My abs tighten. I take a deep breath and sit taller on the couch. I'm rising with her. Flying with her. Landing with—

"Dad! Get out of the way!"

"I don't think so." He sets a television tray in front of me (since when have we owned TV trays?) and grabs the remote off the couch.

"Give it back."

"It's not healthy for you," he says, pressing the power button, and Kate disappears.

I look down at the tray in front of me. A plate overflowing with bites of pre-cut steak, a baked potato with butter *and* sour cream, steamed broccoli, and a warm dinner roll. A glass of milk. Real milk. Two percent by the look of it. And, dear Lord, a brownie. With frosting.

"Watching ski jumping is not healthy for me? But this celebration of cholesterol is? You're joking, right?" I'd push the tray away, but with one gimpy arm I'd probably knock it over. And that steak does smell good.

Dad shakes his head. "I am not joking, and I am not giving the remote back."

He walks into the kitchen, with the remote—the bastard—and returns with a tray for himself. He settles into the chair previously occupied by Jack and cuts off a chunk of steak, pops it in his mouth, and smiles at me. "Mm."

He has no idea how close he is to getting doused with two percent milk. I look where the perfect ammunition to shut him up should be, but it's not there. I pick up the one remote he didn't take away, the one for the sound system, and hit the open button but the CD tray slides out and it's empty.

"Where is it?" I ask.

"Gone," he says, slicing off another bite of steak. "Just like her."

I stare at Dad. Sure, I wake up groggy in the mornings now, hungover from a cocktail of pain relievers with a muscle relaxant chaser, but how could I have not noticed the silencing of Tchaikovsky's second concerto, starring Irina Engebretsen?

It doesn't take long for the answer to come to me. Because my ears have been filled with a different silence.

"So this is how it's going to be now?" I ask Dad. "You, me, eating off TV trays in a dark and quiet room?"

Dad looks out the window. "Doesn't look dark to me."

A month ago the sun would already have set, but there it is, hanging low in the sky and hovering above Lake Superior.

Is there anything time can't change?

I take a bite of my roll and it's sweet, so sweet. I lick my lips and taste butter. Dad, master chef of protein shakes, buttered the top of dinner rolls? I take another bite of my roll. And another. Then a bite of broccoli—also buttered—and then a bite of steak. I even scrape some chocolate frosting off the brownie and lick my finger.

When did I become so hungry?

Dad drags the last quarter of his roll through the bloody meat juice where his steak used to be, then he eats that bit of bread, too, and joins the clean plate club. He moves his tray beside his chair and stretches his good leg in front of him. He rubs his bad knee and grimaces, but then he stretches that leg out as well.

When has Dad ever walked without his cane, much less carried a tray from the kitchen?

He puts his arms behind his head and sighs. I'm ready for a belch that doesn't come. I'm not ready for the words that do.

"Now that we've both had dinner, I thought I'd tell you the news." He stares at his feet. More accurately, at the thick woolen knit socks on his feet. "We've got an appointment tomorrow with an orthopedist in Duluth. It's time we start rehabbing so you can return to competition. Not this year, I know, but next year for sure. We can still make it to PyeongChang, Eleanor, if we work hard enough."

I stare at him. *We* can still make it to PyeongChang if *we* work hard enough?

Clearly, there are some things time can't change.

CHAPTER TWENTY-TWO

T his is most likely a career-ending injury."
That's what Dr. Barlow, the orthopedist at the University Hospital in Duluth, tells us. Neither Dad nor I like Dr. Barlow, but for different reasons. I don't like him because he has bad breath. Dad doesn't like him because he has bad news.

Dad schedules another appointment. This time with Dr. Susan Turner, an orthopedist in Minneapolis who specializes in sports medicine. We have to wait two weeks, but at four in the morning on April 1, Dad piles me into the car and drives to Minneapolis. No joke. I bring my pillow, planning to sleep the five-hour trip, but that doesn't happen. Not with every bump in the road jostling my shoulder and making me want to face-punch Dad. We finally arrive at the University of Minnesota Hospital, and I'm tired, sore, crabby as hell—in no mood for Dr. Turner's sadistically thorough tests. This part of the *we*, I wouldn't mind sharing with Dad.

By two in the afternoon we're sitting in Dr. Turner's office, about to get the results of a physical examination that included flexion and extension, pronation and supination, and strength tests. My shoulder hates Dr. Turner, but I like her. She's quick to smile, has minty-fresh breath, and her physical therapy room has a huge saying painted on the wall that reads, *You gave your all. I'm here to help you get it back.*

"This could be a career-ending injury," Dr. Turner says, and Dad shifts in his chair.

"What do you mean *could be*? Will Eleanor be able to compete by next season or not?"

Dr. Turner doesn't even blink at Dad's rudeness. "Mr. Engebretsen, it's my understanding your ski jumping career was cut short by an injury. Am I correct?"

Dad shakes his head no. Shakes his cane yes. "You don't understand. That was in 1984. There are so many advances in medicine now that we didn't have then. And Eleanor is tough."

Dr. Turner lifts a picture frame off her desk and turns it to face Dad and me. It's a younger Dr. Turner. Her hair is dark, not streaked with gray. She's in her late teens or early twenties and wearing a white leotard with one blue sleeve and one red. It's an action shot that's caught her flying through the air, upside down, from the highest uneven bar to the lowest. Her palms are wrapped in white tape. Her face, focusing beyond the camera, is fierce.

Dad and I look at Dr. Turner with new respect. She comes from our world.

"That picture was taken seconds before my gymnastics career and my Olympic dreams ended, so you see, I do understand." She flashes a smile at me. "And you don't have to tell me Eleanor's tough."

Dr. Turner picks up a sheet of paper. "Eleanor scored five out of five for strength in her right arm and fist. She has full range of motion."

I hear a however coming.

"Passive range of motion is limited by pain in two planes of movement, but more concerning, the strength and coordination of her rotator cuff have been significantly compromised."

Dad stares blankly at Dr. Turner. Like she's talking a foreign language to him, though she's not. Sure, it's a bunch of medical jargon, but what she's saying is obvious. At least to me.

"In other words, my shoulder's seriously fucked up and I'll probably never ski jump again."

"Most athletes would fully recover in time and resume competing," Dr. Turner says.

I hear another however hovering in the room.

"However, Eleanor is a ski jumper, which requires extraordinary torso strength and flexibility. She relies on shoulder stability to extend her arms behind her to act as rudders in the air current."

None of this is news to Dad or me.

"It is unlikely Eleanor will ever regain enough shoulder mobility to jump competitively."

Bam. Talk about laying it out. Next to me, Dad sinks back in his chair.

"However…"

Now that one I didn't see coming.

"However?" Dad lifts his chin to look at Dr. Turner.

"However, *unlikely* isn't the same as *impossible*. I have seen instances when a patient with incredible mental strength was able to overcome physical limitations I thought insurmountable. Mr. Engebretsen, you have a remarkable daughter. If she works hard enough, there is a chance she will jump again."

Jump again, Dr. Turner said. Not compete again. It's a distinction I catch, though it doesn't seem like Dad does.

"Where do we begin, and how soon can we start?" he asks.

We. Still with the *we*.

"She'll need physical therapy three times per week. I also advise daily stretching exercises to increase range of motion and flexibility. Additionally, I'll need to see Eleanor back in one month to monitor her progress and check for any signs of exacerbation to her injuries."

And then, when I'm feeling all warm and fuzzy toward Dr. Turner, she blows it.

"Also, I'd like Eleanor to stop wearing her sling and I'm discontinuing her pain medication."

Just when you think you've found one cool adult.

Dad talks nonstop the entire drive home, mainly on his phone, scheduling physical therapy appointments, authorizing the release of my medical records, planning my big comeback.

Me? I'm exhausted and I haven't even started my rehab regime. Before I know it I'm sound asleep as Dad drives us back to Lutsen.

My routine changes again after the trip to Minneapolis. Actually, it's more like my routine resumes, except jump practice has been replaced by physical therapy. Three times per week Dad drives me to NovaCare Rehabilitation in Lutsen where I work out until I get that hurts-so-good feeling, and in the off days he tries to coach me in gentle stretching, but he speaks the language of vertical thrust and maximum air lift and the only thing getting stretched, frankly, is my patience.

One day I lose it and storm out of the exercise room. It's either that or tie Dad up with the resistance bands he bought on Amazon. Seriously, he read the instructions on the box ten minutes before he began barking them at me.

"Eleanor? Where are you going?" Dad yells after me. "We're not done!"

But I'm done, at least for today, so I grab the keys and take off in the car. I don't have a clue where I'm going, but somehow I end up weaving through the streets of Lutsen until I find myself parked across from Kate's apartment building, staring at the sad little patch of snow in the front yard. It will be gone soon enough, and then there won't be anything left of the winter of Kate.

The door of her apartment opens and I freeze. It's Kate and Turd Ferguson. Kate stands in the front yard, plastic bag in one hand, leash in the other, waiting for Turd to do her business. I crouch down in the car, hopefully low enough Kate can't see me but not so low I can't see her. Her hair looks longer. Maybe an inch, but it looks good on her, especially when the wind blows it. She's wearing jeans and a sweatshirt with Team USA on it. Is that what Kate did instead of visiting me in the hospital? Shop for souvenirs?

Fine. Whatever.

I sit up in the car and turn the key in the ignition. The engine revs, and Kate looks toward the sound. For a second, it's the two of us again—Kate looking into my eyes and me looking into hers. Even though we are fifty feet apart and Turd is living up to her name, I feel something.

Then Kate bends, scoops, and walks toward the front door while Turd, trailing behind her, attempts to kick up every blade of grass she can reach with her hind legs. Kate says something I can't hear and Turd trots over to her. Kate pulls the door open and I watch as the door closes behind them. I briefly consider buzzing her apartment, but I decide I'd rather live with the possibility she might open the door to me than the knowledge she refused.

I drive home. There's no place else to go. Jack's working, and...well, I don't have any other friends. There's Jillian and Linnea and Bogey, but they're not really friends. I mean, we've never hung out or anything. I blame a childhood of private tutors for my stunted social life.

The sky is glowing gold and red when I pull up in front of Gravity Lab and park the car. Upstairs Dad awaits, and the footage of Utah, and probably another green shake for dinner. If I'd known that steak was a one-time thing, I would have eaten it more slowly. I open my car door and breathe in the crisp spring air. Upstairs can wait. I walk out to the jump and climb the steps, all 241 of them. It's been two months since I've looked straight down an inrun and I'm not prepared when the world starts to spin or when my stomach threatens to mutiny.

I sit.

Before I fall.

I grab onto one of the metal poles in the safety gate around the platform until the sparkles float away. Step by step, I climb down the ladder and when I reach the bottom I plop on my ass and try to figure out what the hell just happened.

But I can't, so I go inside and find Dad, upstairs, talking on his phone.

"Great. Thanks so much. We'll see you tomorrow," he says and then hangs up.

I'd ask. If I cared.

If my mind weren't stuck on top of the jump, spinning like a kaleidoscope and distorting everything I thought I saw clearly.

"Are you hungry?" Dad asks. "I could order pizza."

It's a lame peace offering and we both know it.

"I ate in town." I walk down the hall to my bedroom and close the door behind me. The truth is I wouldn't trust my stomach with pizza. Or anything else. I lie on the bed. My room wobbles. I close my eyes and roll onto my right side. Will I ever lie on my left side again? There are so many things I don't know.

I fall asleep in my clothes. I don't remember falling asleep, but it's dark when my pocket buzzes me awake. I'm about to decide it was a dream when it happens again and I realize my cell phone is vibrating. Probably Jack, texting me about another hot girl. I pull it out and swipe the screen.

Hey, the text reads. That's it, but it's enough to make me sit straight up in bed and stare at the three letters shining in the darkness.

Hey yourself, I text back. *I miss you.*

Slow down, El. Put on the brakes. You blew the trial. Don't fuck up again.

Three minutes later I ignore my own advice. *And I am so sorry. Can we talk?*

I stay up for two hours, waiting for a response that never comes, and when I fall back asleep I am certain that I have blown it again.

❖

"Eleanor? Time to get up!" Dad's voice bellows through the door of my room and I crack open my eyes. Nine a.m.? Since when do I need to be up at nine a.m.? My physical therapy appointments are at one.

I roll onto my back and ignore him.

I'm dozing off again when he knocks on my door. "We've got an appointment. Time to get up."

I sit up. Consider throwing the pillow. Decide against it. Remember the text. Pull my phone out. Make sure it really happened. Confirm that it did. There's no going back to sleep after all that, so I get up and haul my sleepy ass into the bathroom. Twenty minutes later I emerge and find Dad in the living room, holding the car keys.

"Ready to go?"

I'd ask. If I cared.

"Sure."

We're in the car, driving toward Lutsen, when I decide Dad's rescheduled my physical therapy appointment to the morning for some ungodly reason. I groan.

Dad stops at Main Street and hits his blinker. Yep. NovaCare, here I come. But then he turns right. I shoot a look at him, but he's hiding behind his stupid mirrored sunglasses and staring straight ahead. And then I don't need to ask because he pulls up and I'm staring at a sight I can't believe.

"Now, before you refuse," he says. "I asked, and you'll have the whole place to yourself. She agreed to private lessons in return for the cost of..." His voice trails off, but I know how that sentence ends. In return for the cost of the jumpsuit, the goggles, the gloves, and the skis. No, the skis were a gift, but the rest was on an installment plan. "I checked with Dr. Turner and told her I don't know what I'm doing to help with gentle stretching, and she suggested yoga. So?" he asks.

I remember what she said on the night John Mellencamp tried to sing truth into me with his voice full of smoke and broken mirrors.

Oh, and Eleanor? Do not, under any circumstance, disrespect my daughter.

First the text, the goddamn indecipherable text. Meant for my eyes. Never to be unread.

And now Maggie.

CHAPTER TWENTY-THREE

If there were a sun salutation called *Facing the Music* or a yoga pose called *Stomach Tied in Knots* I'd be the yogini and Maggie would be the student.

But there's not.

So I walk into Flex Appeal to be stretched, hopefully gently, by Kate's mom.

Class has just ended and there are all forms of yoga-panted women—*hello*—and a few yoga-panted men—*ew*—putting on shoes and coats and getting ready to leave. I try to blend in with the sea of spandex for as long as possible, but eventually I'm the last person in the studio other than Maggie, who is moving quietly, her bare feet making no sound on the floors she and I stained together when things were right between us. Or at least, less wrong. Maggie doesn't look at me or speak to me as she sets up what I assume is the yoga mat meant for me directly across from hers. I watch her arranging foam blocks on my mat and wonder what I should do. Break the silence? Go straight for the, *Hey Maggie, good to see you*, and pretend I didn't treat Kate like shit? Or should I come right out with it and say I'm sorry? What does that even sound like? *Hey, Maggie, I'm sorry I lied to Kate during our whole relationship, but I did love her. Toward the end, at least.*

Fuck. I'd throw my ass out of the studio. Why wouldn't Maggie?

I wander over to the reception area to check out all the bizarre and beautiful things Maggie has done to make Flex Appeal the coolest, by far, yoga studio in the history of yoga studios. Who saws a claw-footed bathtub in half and turns it into a couch, complete with a custom-made cushion? Who screws legs into the base of an old suitcase and turns it into a table? Who hangs wooden ladders horizontally on the wall to make bookshelves? Only Maggie.

I wander over to check out the ladder-shelves and scan the odd assortment of books on topics like living a Zen life and looking for your life's repurpose. There's even a book called *Wabi Sabi* with a bowl on the cover I assume is a sushi cookbook. There's a whole section on yoga with titles containing words I don't have a clue how to pronounce. Ananda, Hatha, Jivamukti, Kundalini, Vinyasa. Apparently yoga is having a love affair with vowels.

"Are you ready, Ellie?" Maggie appears in the doorway. She doesn't look mad.

I nod, take off my shoes, and follow Maggie into the studio where music, not Tchaikovsky and not John Mellencamp, is playing softly in the background. There's a wood instrument and possibly a rain stick. Or maybe real rain. Maybe it's a Buddhist monk on top of a mountain playing a wooden flute in the rain.

Maggie sits on her mat and makes a pretzel of her legs. Beside her a towel is covering something. No clue what, but then this is yoga, so it's all pretty much a mystery to me. I sit and pretzel my legs, too. Not as perfectly as Maggie though because my hamstrings have gotten tight from sitting on my ass for two months.

Maggie brings her hands to her chest, palms together, and closes her eyes. I mirror Maggie, feel silly, and note the dull tug in my left shoulder blade. Lifting my arms to my chest is bearable. Over my head? No fucking way.

Maggie takes a deep breath and exhales. And another. "Breath is life, Ellie." Maggie's voice is so soft it's more of a whisper. "Breathe life into your body."

I breathe. In and out. In and out. This, my body remembers.

"Good. Let's begin with a guided meditation. Are you able to lie on your back?"

I open my eyes to find Maggie looking at me. I don't know what's worse, the kindness I don't deserve or the eighth of an inch of foam between me and the hardwood floor.

"I'll try." I put my right hand behind me and lower myself as slowly as possible, but pain explodes in my left shoulder blade the minute it feels the weight of my body.

"Fuck!" I try to push myself up with my right arm, but that doesn't work so I add my left which is as dumb as it gets. The pain doubles.

"Oh, fuck!" I'm floundering and heading for a crash onto the floor, but then Maggie is behind me, propping me up with her arms.

When did she move?

And why is she helping me?

"I'm so sorry, Maggie. I'm so fucking sorry." Tears burn down my cheeks as I go limp in her arms.

She helps me into a seated position and sits next to me, which is good. Side by side, I don't have to look into her eyes and she doesn't have to look into mine.

"I believe you," she says, whisper-soft again. "There's not much worse in life than being hurt so badly you lose yourself and wind up hurting someone you love, is there?"

I can't breathe. I'm hiccup-sobbing and drowning in pain, not one bit of it from my shoulder blade. "Unless you're the person who gets hurt by the lost person."

Maggie sighs. "There is that."

She moves back to her mat when I'm done dripping tears all over her. She places whatever is under that towel between us, lifts the cloth, and I find myself looking at a bowl, her bowl, the one with the roses and the ivy, the bowl she inherited from her mother, the bowl I dropped on the floor and broke. Except it's not broken anymore. It's pieced back together with some kind of dark yellow glue that weaves in and out of the ivy and makes a few of the rose petals shine.

"Do you remember this?" she asks, and I nod. Feel even more miserable, though I didn't think that was possible.

"Have you ever heard of wabi sabi?"

"The hot green stuff on sushi that clears your sinuses? Yeah. Why?" I have no idea what sushi has to do with broken bones or broken hearts or broken bowls.

Maggie smiles at me. "You're thinking wasabi, Ellie. I'm talking about wabi sabi, the Japanese art form and philosophy." I stare at her blankly and she continues. "The concept began with a Japanese potter who would throw pots and put them in a kiln where many would break. Other potters would toss their broken pieces, but he kept his and eventually patched them together with the medium of gold, making the bowls stronger and more valuable because they had once been broken."

I look at the dark yellow glue that isn't glue. At the bowl that is no longer broken. "So I didn't ruin your bowl?"

Maggie shakes her head and I'm pretty sure she knows by *bowl* I mean *daughter*. "Broke it? Yes. Ruined? No. My turn to ask you a question. Can a broken bowl glue itself back together?"

I shake my head.

"Can one broken bowl mend another broken bowl?"

"Of course not," I answer. I half expect Maggie to haul out the Humpty Dumpty story, but she doesn't.

"Then all we can do is acknowledge the brokenness in ourselves and in others, leave our bowls in the potter's hands, and trust he's going to bring the gold."

Bring the gold. That always meant something else to me. Like fulfilling a father's expectations. With Maggie, I see it could mean something more.

She straightens her back and turns her face toward the ceiling. "Now let's begin our meditation, but from a seated position. I'd like you to close your eyes and listen to my voice as I move your attention from one place in your body to another. Feel your strength. Allow your pain to surface, and when it does, visualize yourself holding your broken places in your hands and sealing them together with gold, okay?"

I nod, close my eyes, and Maggie begins with my toes, moves to my ankles, then my calves, and everything is going fine until she gets to my ribs that surround my heart and I can't help but wonder whether Maggie can afford all the gold it's going to take to piece that together.

After the guided meditation, Maggie moves me through some yoga poses—nothing too ambitious for a former Olympic hopeful ski jumper. I handle the Warrior Pose II fine. Even feel a little badass doing it. I sail through the Eagle Pose. I twist with Bharadvajasana and am settling into the Mountain Pose when I hear the front door open, the sound of footsteps, a voice saying, "Hey, Mom! I'm here. You ready for our celebration lunch?" and I remember the last time I was a poser in the shadow of a mountain.

Yoga with Maggie comes to an abrupt end.

Kate walks into the studio and, lucky me, I get to watch the happiness drain off her face.

Maggie ignores the tension and begins rolling up her mat. "Sorry, hon. I can't get away today. Why don't you and Ellie go out for lunch? You know, before you—"

"Mom." There's an edge in Kate's voice that shuts Maggie up. Kate turns to me. "What are you doing here?"

"I'm, ah…here for, um…"

Maggie saves my butt. "She's here for yoga. What else?"

"And it's a total coincidence *you* told me to be here right as *her* class is ending and now *you* can't go to lunch with me but *Ellie* can?"

"Yes." Maggie tosses the towel in the wabi sabi bowl and stares Kate down. "A complete coincidence. And now I'm kicking you out because my next class begins in ten minutes." She waves her hand like she's shooing us out of the studio, which she is.

I offer Kate a way out. It's the least I can do. "Dad is coming back for me soon."

"I'm afraid he isn't." Maggie doesn't even try to hide her grin. "I told him Kate would drive you home. Now get out of here, you two, and have a nice lunch."

The dining options are mainly at the ski resort where everything between us began. Kate hesitates at the end of the road that connects with Highway 61, then turns her car toward Lutsen. She parks in the same lot where Jack tricked her into filling out a satisfaction survey so I could have her number. Is it possible that happened this past January? Can a person live a lifetime in four months? I get out of the car and turn toward Rosie's Chalet automatically, but Kate walks past Rosie's.

"Where are you going?" I ask.

She points at the gondola that leads to the top of Moose Mountain. "I think we should aim higher this time, don't you?"

I follow Kate, walking past the landscaping crew that is raking decaying leaves off the ground saturated from the melted snow. The resort, like everyone else in Lutsen it seems, is midtransition. The chill has passed with the ski season, but warmth hasn't settled in enough to attract the summer tourists who come here for the waterslide.

Kate walks through the empty line for the gondola, which is free with a ski season pass but costs fifteen dollars per person during the summer.

"We have to buy tickets in the gift shop," I tell Kate. My season pass would get us a free ride, but it's at home since I didn't wake up this morning planning on riding to the top of a mountain with Kate Moreau.

"Naw, you're good, El." The gondola operator, whose name I should know but don't, says to me. He guides the gondola around to us and opens the door. "That was a helluva fall. Almost crapped my pants when I saw it on ESPN. You okay, Ellie? You're going to compete again, aren't you?"

Kate steps in the gondola and claims the seat facing the mountain.

"Which question do you want me to answer?" I ask.

"You look okay, so I guess whether or not you're going to compete again. You're Lutsen's claim to fame, you know."

Yes. Yes, I know.

"Not sure yet." I step into the red cab, hesitate for a second, and then sit in the seat across from Kate. "Thanks for the ride."

"Anytime." He nods and closes the door.

And I instantly regret my decision. Side by side worked well with Maggie. It allowed for the whole honest-without-the-pressure-of-eye-contact dynamic. What was I thinking? Oh yeah, that Kate probably didn't want my body pressed up against hers on the small seat stupidly built for one and a half people.

We opt for awkward silence.

I swivel around to look at the mountain stripped naked of snow. It's a sight that shocks me every spring, because it's the only time the damage is laid bare. Downed trees. Hills sculpted in some areas with bulldozers. Built up in others with piles of dirt. In a month the trees will be firewood and an inch of grass will cover the exposed black soil with a stubble of green.

The tail end of Valley Run passes beneath us, and in the distance I spot the jump on Mogen Terrain Park where I fell and Kate picked me up.

"Weird, huh?" I turn to ask Kate.

"Very." She nods.

We bump to a stop at the top of Moose Mountain and climb out of the gondola, where I have an almost identical conversation about my accident with another operator whose name I don't know. "Not sure yet," I answer when he asks when I'm returning to competition and a look of sadness flashes across Kate's face.

We leave the gondola station and are walking toward Summit Chalet when Kate stops abruptly. "Damn," she says as she stares at Lake Superior, for once taking the time to appreciate the view, and I remember this is her first look at the lake when it's not covered with snow or ice.

"That right there is the best part of the top of Moose Mountain," I tell her.

"What comes in second?"

"The chili cheese Tater Tots at Summit Chalet. They're killer." I leave Kate to soak up the view as long as she wants and walk into the chalet where I endure conversation number three about my accident with the waitress who cracks a joke about a ski jumper who finds her competition status up in the air.

So not funny.

I order two large chili cheese Tater Tots and sodas and wait for Kate who walks in as the food arrives. We head outside to eat on the deck where the view is even better, and it becomes clear I'm going to have to compete with a Great Lake for Kate's attention.

I pick at the Tater Tots, lick my fingers, and watch Kate stare past me. We are the only two people at Summit Chalet, which makes everything feel even weirder. Sort of like we came here to have a conversation so important, so private, it could only take place on the top of a deserted mountain.

I know what I need to say, but not how to say it. Though as the silence between us stretches almost as far as Lake Superior, I figure out Kate is going to make me talk first. Which is only fair, all things considered. She's been incredibly generous not making me wear her chili cheese Tater Tots so far. "I fucked up," I blurt out when nothing else comes to me.

Kate pulls her gaze off the lake and stares at me blankly for the longest minute in the history of minutes. "How?"

Crap.

"I wasn't honest with you and I should have been." I was wrong. That minute before was the second longest minute in the history of minutes.

"Why?" Her stare is no longer blank. She's sketched in a bunch of pain and a smidge of anger.

Double crap.

I run my hand through my hair and immediately wish I'd wiped my fingers on a napkin first. I force myself to look her in the eyes. She deserves that much at least. "Because I wasn't being honest with myself."

"About?"

This one is easier. This answer I know. "You, Kate. I wasn't admitting to myself that I was falling for you the whole time."

Dead air. Which I interpret to mean she would like me to elaborate.

"I was scared. I know that sounds like an excuse, but it's the truth. I had lost two people I thought I'd never lose. If I had faced the fact that I was falling in love with you, I would have also had to face the possibility of losing you and I couldn't do that."

Kate nods. "That's what she told me."

"She who?"

"Blair." Kate turns to gaze at the lake for a bit.

I am suddenly no longer hungry. "Wait. Blair went to see you?"

Kate nods. "Called. Texted. Finally tracked me down and stood on the front yard shouting at me until I let her in. I almost sicced Turd Ferguson on her. Your ex is a huge pain in the ass."

I laugh. Can't help it. "Tell me about it."

"I'd say you have terrible taste in women, but—"

"You're wrong," I interrupt. "I don't have taste in women at all anymore." Kate raises an eyebrow and I realize I sound like I've chucked my whole Say No To Dick policy, which could not be further from the truth. "What I mean is there are no other women for me anymore. Except you."

Kate blows right past what should have been the perfect make-up moment. "Do you want to hear what Blair had to say or not?"

This has to be a trick question, right? Saying yes could be interpreted as me showing interest in Blair, but saying no could shut the conversation down, and Kate is finally talking to me again. This is going to take an approach I'm not used to.

The truth.

"Only if she told you I am crazy in love with you," I tell Kate. "If she said anything else, she's a liar, and I don't want to ever hear her name again unless you tell me Turd peed on her leg, because I'd love to hear that story."

Kate laughs. Progress. I chalk one up to truth. "She pretty much said what you said. That you had told her you were happier than you've ever been because of me right before I walked in on the two of you with your hands all over each other."

"She said we had our hands all over each other?" I shout, not that it matters. It's only Kate and me and the mountain and Lake Superior.

"I may have added that part." Kate fills in the pain sketch on her face with a few more subtle shades.

"Don't. Please don't. That never happened. You have to believe me."

Kate erases some of the hurt, but she doesn't wipe the slate clean. "You gave up the right to tell me what to believe, El. I'm going to need time to think and figure out how I feel."

"Take it," I rush in. "As much as you need."

Kate smiles, not warmly. "Oh, I was planning to, but I do appreciate you giving me permission."

It feels like a conversation killer, and I'm sitting there, wondering how I managed to dig myself into a deeper hole, when Kate drops a bomb on me.

"I'm leaving in the morning, El."

And I thought Blair bombarding Kate was the surprise. "Leaving? What are you talking about? Where are you going?"

Kate reaches for her purse, takes out a letter, and sets it on the table in front of me. I recognize the logo next to the return address. "I'm meeting with the coach next week. If they like what they see, I may make the cut."

I pick up the letter and read three words before tears fill my eyes. Utah Olympic Park. "Oh my God, Kate! The Women's U.S. National Ski Jumping team? Are you serious?" The tears fall but I don't even care, I'm so happy for her.

"I'm sure it would have been you," she says, misunderstanding my waterworks display entirely. "If you hadn't fallen."

But I don't even care about that. Kate is trying out for the freaking U.S. National Ski Jumping team! I'm out of my chair and coming at her and then she's in my arms and I'm trying to lift her off the ground and failing miserably because of my stupid shoulder and then I'm wincing and she's holding me and my tears are part pain, part joy. Mostly joy.

"I am so fucking proud of you," I tell her, and I chalk another one up for truth, because I see her again, my Kate, face plastered to a plane window, setting her sights on a new horizon. It's probably way too fast and assuming too much, but she's already in my arms and she's going to be gone tomorrow. I take her face in my hands and kiss her and she doesn't pull away.

"It feels like a dream," Kate whispers. "Except in a real dream, you'd be there with me."

"Oh, I will be," I tell her. "As soon as I can."

The question she doesn't want to ask is written all over her face.

"I will be there, Kate. Whether I'm the head of your fan club or your teammate. I promise."

Kate reaches up and touches my collarbone. Reaches behind and runs her hand over my shoulder blade. "Are you going to be okay, El?"

"I'm not sure yet," I tell her. "It depends."

"On?"

"Us."

Kate grins. Takes my hand in hers. "Us, huh? What if I say we are definitely *not not* okay."

"Then I'd say I'm damn lucky," I tell her and decide by the smile on her face that I could get used to this whole telling the truth approach.

PART V: THE TELEMARK

One foot in front of the other, that's the way to land.
One foot in front of the other, that's the way to move forward.

CHAPTER TWENTY-FOUR

Throughout the rest of the spring and long into the summer I work with Maggie at Flex Appeal while Kate, after a brief and glorious tryout, trains with the National Team for the upcoming jumping season. I miss her like hell, but this is her time to test her wings as much as it is mine.

One day, long after Kate's bill at Gravity Lab has been settled through private yoga lessons, I'm hanging out at Flex Appeal because I want to be there and Maggie hasn't tossed me out the door yet. She's between classes and tsk-tsking at the path worn dull in the dark walnut where hundreds of feet have walked and hundreds of people have healed. It's been a busy summer, which is good for business. Bad for floors.

Maggie turns to me. "What are you doing this weekend?"

It took being broken to receive the first bit of wisdom Maggie gave me on the day we met, and it's about time I thank her, even if it means spending the day on my knees, working my shoulder out. "Practicing what you've taught me to do this summer. Stripping off the old, sanding down to the grain, and applying a new stain."

Maggie's smile blossoms on her face. "Meet you here Saturday morning at nine?"

"Can't think of anywhere I'd rather be." That may be a breach of my new Truth Only policy because there is somewhere I'd rather be, unless Kate were to come home for a big floor fixing party with Maggie and me. Then it would be the God's honest truth.

But she doesn't, so Maggie and I re-stain the floors and it feels right, the two of us doing the work together. This time we even remember to begin at the back of the studio.

The leaves on the trees by the jump at Gravity Lab get a new stain job, too. Deep crimson, gold, orange. Until they fly away and take their beauty with them. It's a crappy pattern I've come to accept. One day I wake up to the sight of snowflakes swirling outside my bedroom window and feel the familiar tug, the one that pulls against gravity and allows me to fly. I can practically smell the snow in the air at the top of the jump. I walk into the living room and grab my jacket, head toward the staircase.

"Going somewhere?" Dad asks. The cup of coffee in his hands is steaming.

"I'll be back soon." It's all the answer I can give him because that's what I'm going outside to discover: if I'm going to try to go anywhere or not.

It's colder than I expected. I pull my ski gloves out of my coat pockets where I left them a lifetime ago and slide them over my hands. They're soft and broken in and perfect. I cross the yard and climb the ladder to the jump again, sit on the platform, and look down the inrun. The world still wobbles a little, but not as much, and I'm sitting there, waiting for it to settle into place, when I hear the ladder groan under another person's weight. Bogey? Probably. Snow calls him to Gravity Lab like a homing pigeon returning to his roost. Though it could be Linnea or Jillian. Probably not Geoffrey-with-a-*G* or Blair. Rumor has it, they broke up.

"Eleanor?" Dad's voice startles me. "Want some company?" I can't remember a time when Dad actually climbed up to the jump. Shouted at it from the coach's stand? Sure. Directed it like a guy in a tuxedo waving a wand in front of an orchestra? Ad nauseam. Climbed it himself? Not once that I recall.

"Dad?" I lean over the ladder and watch him balance on his bum leg in order to take another step with his good leg, only to pull his bum leg up to that step and repeat the whole process. Two hundred forty-one times.

"How are you going to get back down?" I ask, and he laughs a cloud of overconfidence into the air.

"Not sure, but we'll figure it out."

Again with the *we*. I didn't tell him to haul his gimpy ass up my jump.

His knuckles are white when they grip the bar at the top of the ladder. His face is even whiter when he half pulls-half lunges his body onto the platform and sits beside me.

"Oof." He checks out the view and grabs the same metal pole in the safety gate I grabbed two months ago. I wonder how much the world wobbles after twenty years.

We sit there for a while, watching snow collect on the start bar, in the grooves of the inrun, on each other's head. This is probably the moment I've been anticipating, though I imagined he and I would be sitting on the couch with his laptop between us and the FIS ski website pulled up. I should have learned by now nothing happens the way I imagine it will.

"So?" he asks.

"Soon," I tell him. "Not today."

He sighs out a long foggy stream of frustration.

It's time. I know it is.

"Dad?" I ask though not much more than a puff of air accompanies the question. It's going to take a helluva lot more steam behind my words if I'm going to be heard. I take a deep breath and blow it out hard.

"What is it, Eleanor? Just tell me," Dad says, when my courage cloud dissipates.

"I still want to compete and I want to go for the National Team and then the Olympics." He starts to say something. Probably hallelujah, but I stop him. "The thing is..." How do I tell Dad his dream is too heavy and I can't fly with it anymore? How does a daughter break her father's heart? I take another deep breath. Breathe out another cloud of confidence. "Even if I make it to PyeongChang, there's not going to be any Engebretsen gold. I need you to understand that, Dad."

He stares at me for a few seconds and then his face plays all his emotions like a movie set to fast-forward. Confusion. Shock. Understanding. Hurt.

"I'm sorry," I tell him. "I know you're disappointed in me." A tear slides down my cheek, but Dad wipes it away before it can freeze there.

His face plays the last emotion, something that looks an awful lot like love. "You can never disappoint me, Ellie. Don't you know that? You've been my Engebretsen gold since the day you were born." His ice-blue eyes shine as he looks at me.

I take another look down the inrun and everything is where it should be. The sky. The ground. Everything in between. Not one bit of it is wobbling.

Time may not change everything, but it does reveal everything.

EPILOGUE

Two Years Later
PyeongChang, South Korea

Maggie was right. The parrot training school is cool, and I buy a postcard with two parrots sitting on a branch like lovebirds for 3,529.29 KRW in the gift shop.

Dear Maggie, I write on the back of the postcard.

> *Did you know a parrot can learn to say over one thousand words? You do now.*
> *Guess what? Kate only needed to say one word, but she chose a beautiful word.*
> *Yes.*
> *She said yes!*
> *El*

PS, Kate writes, *First and last time I'm going to admit it. Mom, you were right. El and I are perfect for each other. Love you, K*

I pay 11,764.31 KRW to mail the postcard to the United States, and Maggie will still beat it home, but the look on her face when she gets the postcard will be priceless. At least Kate and I think it will be.

That's how torches are passed. A postcard tradition from one person to another. A flame from one runner to another. Until everything, all over the world, is lit up with love.

Kate shouts something at me as we walk onto the running track inside the stadium at PyeongChang.

"What?" I yell at her, cupping my hand behind my ear. She points at the stadium filled with thousands and thousands of people.

"Do you see them?" she shouts, and I laugh, but I look anyway. There's nothing I wouldn't do for this woman, this amazing woman, who has agreed to move in with me. My season of rehab is finally over, which means I'll be a twenty-year-old college freshman at the University of Utah next fall, being bored silly by a bunch of core classes, while Kate, a junior, will be studying her passion: behavioral mental health, specializing in addiction recovery. One way or another, I figure, she's still trying to save her dad.

I follow her gaze. "Yep." I point. Somewhere. "Third row from the top. Section 1,453. Seats M and N." Kate spoils me with my favorite sound, her laughter, and pulls me close. "Your mom is on the left. Dad's on the right." I squint. "Nope. Other way around."

I could go on all day, making Kate laugh, but there are laps to take and jumps to make and records to break.

Kate smiles and loops her arm through mine. I reach for my teammate beside me as Kate reaches for the girl next to her. "PyeongChang, here we come!" Kate shouts. She leads us forward as one star-spangled team through the swaying masses that are separated by country, color, and sport, but united in spirit. "And may the best woman win!"

I'll let the judges decide who gets the medals, but I already know who's won.

Me.

Author's Note: The Real Heroes

While Eleanor Engebretsen and Kate Moreau are fictional characters, the struggle for women ski jumpers to be allowed to compete in the Olympics, as referenced in this book, is a very real part of the sport's history. In 2010, a lawsuit was filed by fifteen female ski jumpers against the IOC on the basis of gender discrimination, and though the suit was defeated, public relations pressure eventually caused the IOC to reverse their decision and allow women's ski jumping as an Olympic sport.

American ski jumper Sarah Hendrickson, who so generously answered my many questions and fact-checked *Gravity* throughout the stages of drafting and revision, made history in Sochi in 2014 when she became the first female ski jumper to ever compete in the Olympics. Though the Olympic barrier has been breached, the struggle to find equal footing continues. Currently women ski jumpers are allowed to compete in one event while their male counterparts compete in three. Funding remains a critical issue and athletes rely on endorsement money, crowd-funding, and private donations. This is especially true in the United States, where the sport does not garner the attention it deserves.

To support the sport of women's ski jumping, please visit the website of Women's Ski Jumping USA, a nonprofit 501(c)(3) organization, at wsjusa.com.

This book was inspired by and is dedicated to every woman who has ever dared to fly free.

About the Author

Minnesota writer Juliann Rich spent her childhood in search of the perfect climbing tree. The taller, the better! A branch thirty feet off the ground and surrounded by leaves, caterpillars, birds, and squirrels was a good perch for a young girl to find herself. Seeking truth in nature and finding a unique point of view remain crucial elements in her life as well as her writing.

Juliann is the author of four affirming young adult novels: *Caught in the Crossfire, Searching for Grace, Taking the Stand*, and *Gravity*. She writes character-driven books about young adults who are bound to discover their true selves and the courage to create an authentic life…if the journey doesn't break them.

Juliann is the 2014 recipient of the Emerging Writer Award from The Saints and Sinners Literary Festival and lives with her husband and an adorable but naughty dachshund named Bella in a quaint 1920s brownstone in Minneapolis.

Visit her at www.juliannrich.com.

Soliloquy Titles From Bold Strokes Books

Gravity by Juliann Rich. How can Ellie Engebretsen, Olympic ski jumping hopeful with her eye on the gold, soar through the air when all she feels like doing is falling hard for Kate Moreau, her greatest competitor and the girl of her dreams? (978-1-62639-483-4)

18 Months by Samantha Boyette. Alissa Reeves has only had two girlfriends and they've both gone missing. Now it's up to her to find out why. (978-1-62639-804-7)

Before by KE Payne. When Tally falls in love with her band's new recruit, she has a tough decision to make. What does she want more—Alex or the band? (978-1-62639-677-7)

Banished Sons Of Poseidon by Andrew J. Peters. Escaped to an underworld of magical wonders and warring, aboriginal peoples, an outlaw priest named Dam must undertake a desperate mission to bring the survivors of Atlantis home. (978-1-62639-441-4)

Breaking Up Point by Brian McNamara. Brendan and Mark may have managed to keep their relationship a secret, but what will happen when they find themselves miles apart as Brendan embarks on his college journey? (978-1-62639-430-8)

The Orion Mask by Greg Herren. After his father's death, Heath comes to Louisiana to meet his mother's family and learn the truth about her death—but some secrets can prove deadly. (978-1-62639-355-4)

The First Twenty by Jennifer Lavoie. Peyton is out for revenge after her father is murdered by Scavengers, but after meeting Nixie, she's torn between helping the girl she loves and the community that raised her. (978-1-62639-414-8)

Taking the Stand by Juliann Rich. There's a time for justice, then there's a time for taking the stand. And Jonathan Cooper knows exactly what time it is. (978-1-62639-408-7)

Dark Rites by Jeremy Jordan King. When friends start experimenting with dark magic to gain power, Margarite must embrace her natural gifts to save them. (978-1-62639-245-8)

Driving Lessons by Annameekee Hesik. Dive into Abbey Brooks's sophomore year as she attempts to figure out the amazing, but sometimes complicated, life of a you-know-who girl at Gila High School. (978-1-62639-228-1)

Asher's Shot by Elizabeth Wheeler. Asher Price's candid photographs capture the truth, but when his success requires exposing an enemy, Asher discovers his only shot at happiness involves revealing secrets of his own. (978-1-62639-229-8)

The Melody of Light by M.L. Rice. After surviving abuse and loss, will Riley Gordon be able to navigate her first year of college and accept true love and family? (78-1-62639-219-9)

Maxine Wore Black by Nora Olsen. Jayla will do anything for Maxine, the girl of her dreams, but after becoming ensnared in Maxine's dark secrets, she'll have to choose between love and her own life. (978-1-62639-208-3)

Bottled Up Secret by Brian McNamara. When Brendan Madden befriends his gorgeous, athletic classmate, Mark, it doesn't take long for Brendan to fall head over heels for him—but will Mark reciprocate the feelings? (978-1-62639-209-0)

Searching for Grace by Juliann Rich. First it's a rumor. Then it's a fact. And then it's on. (978-1-62639-196-3)

Dark Tide by Greg Herren. A summer working as a lifeguard at a hotel on the Gulf Coast seems like a dream job…until Ricky Hackworth realizes the town is shielding some very dark—and deadly—secrets. (978-1-62639-197-0)

Everything Changes by Samantha Hale. Raven Walker's world is turned upside down the moment Morgan O'Shea walks into her life. (978-1-62639-303-5)

Fifty Yards and Holding by David Matthew-Barnes. The discovery of a secret relationship between Riley Brewer, the star of the high school baseball team, and Victor Alvarez, the leader of a violent street gang, escalates into a preventable tragedy. (978-1-62639-081-2)

Caught in the Crossfire by Juliann Rich. Two boys at Bible camp; one forbidden love. (978-1-62639-070-6)

Tristant and Elijah by Jennifer Lavoie. After Elijah finds a scandalous letter belonging to Tristant's great-uncle, the boys set out to discover the secret Uncle Glenn kept hidden his entire life and end up discovering who they are in the process. (978-1-62639-075-1)

Frenemy of the People by Nora Olsen. Clarissa and Lexie have despised each other for as long as they can remember, but when they both find themselves helping an unlikely contender for homecoming queen, they are catapulted into an unexpected romance. (978-1-62639-063-8)

The Balance by Neal Wooten. Love and survival come together in the distant future as Piri and Niko face off against the worst factions of mankind's evolution. (978-1-62639-055-3)

The Unwanted by Jeffrey Ricker. Jamie Thomas is plunged into danger when he discovers his mother is an Amazon who needs his help to save the tribe from a vengeful god. (978-1-62639-048-5)

Because of Her by KE Payne. When Tabby Morton is forced to move to London, she's convinced her life will never be the same again. But the beautiful and intriguing Eden Palmer is about to show her that this time, change is most definitely for the better. (978-1-62639-049-2)

Asher's Fault by Elizabeth Wheeler. Fourteen-year-old Asher Price sees the world in black and white, much like the photos he takes, but when his little brother drowns at the same moment Asher experiences his first same-sex kiss, he can no longer hide behind the lens of his camera and eventually discovers he isn't the only one with a secret. (978-1-60282-982-4)

The Seventh Pleiade by Andrew J. Peters. When Atlantis is besieged by violent storms, tremors, and a barbarian army, it will be up to a young gay prince to find a way for the kingdom's survival. (978-1-60282-960-2)

Meeting Chance by Jennifer Lavoie. When man's best friend turns on Aaron Cassidy, the teen keeps his distance until fate puts Chance in his hands. (978-1-60282-952-7)

Lake Thirteen by Greg Herren. A visit to an old cemetery seems like fun to a group of five teenagers, who soon learn that sometimes it's best to leave old ghosts alone. (978-1-60282-894-0)

The Road to Her by KE Payne. Sparks fly when actress Holly Croft, star of UK soap *Portobello Road*, meets her new on-screen love interest, the enigmatic and sexy Elise Manford. (978-1-60282-887-2)

Swans and Clons by Nora Olsen. In a future world where there are no males, sixteen-year-old Rubric and her girlfriend Salmon Jo must fight to survive when everything they believed in turns out to be a lie. (978-1-60282-874-2)